Black Lightning

Seven Secret Wives

Jo Hammers
Paranormal Crossroads & Publishing

Black Lightning, Seven Secret Wives

Copyright © 2011 by Jo Hammers

ISBN 978-0-9849879-9-3

www.paranormalcrossroads.com

This work is fiction. All of the characters, organizations, and events portrayed in this novel are either products of the author's imagination or are used fictitiously.

Cover Art by Jo Hammers, 2011.

Table of Contents

Black Lightning

Seven Secret Wives

Jo Hammers

Paranormal Crossroads & Publishing

CHAPTER ONE

The Death Angel's Mission

Osceola Black Lightning, a death angel, had been transporting souls for many years from planet Earth to God's Heaven. She was what she was, and set in her ways. In Heaven, she was known as an angel that you did not mess with. Osceola took her job seriously and was not past reaping any soul that got in the way of her assigned missions, whether it was their time to cross over or not.

Transporting souls from disasters was her specialty. She was not a wimpy angel like guardian angels. They had one individual assigned to them. Osceola had been known to escort hundreds of souls over at one crossing. She was a one woman death angel army who feared nothing, including having serious confrontations with God on various subjects.

Osceola had been summoned by God for a new assignment. She was soon to be promoted to guarding the Eastern Gate of Heaven where thousands of souls entered every day. Her upcoming promotion was not to her liking. It would end her Earth travel and shopping trips in New York City and Paris. She was a well dressed, black skinned, death angel who wore designer clothing, diamonds, and stilettos. She was not looking forward to being stuck on a gate, having to carry her lunch, and putting up with mouthy first timers entering Heaven. As a death angel, she had free time on Earth to do what she wanted while she was waiting on someone to take their last breath. Her job as a death angel didn't start till they let go of life. On the in-between, she shopped, had her nails done, and hung out in the back rooms of upcoming fashion designers, although she was invisible to them. She was always number one on Heaven's best dressed angel list. Her promotion to guarding the Eastern Gate would end that.

"Good morning, Osceola!" God greeted her. He was smiling from ear to ear like a Cheshire cat as he stood in his garden leaning against the trunk of a flowering paradise tree. "That is one great looking designer hat you have on! Is it new?"

"Don't go complementing me on my hat, God. When you brown nose me like that, I know you are about to lay one awful assignment on me that no one else wants. Am I right?" Osceola Black Lightning asked in her syrupy, sticky, sweet fly catching voice.

Osceola Black Lightning was a black skinned woman weighing at least three hundred pounds, but stunningly dressed. She had on a gold mesh hat with strings of pearls looping down around its edge. Naturally, she carried a gold bag mesh bag to match. On her feet were eye blinding, gold, open toed stilettos revealing bright red painted toenails. On Earth she would have looked like she was dressed for some great event or ball. In Heaven, it was her everyday clothes. Some angels liked silver, her preference was gold. She wasn't too keen on the pearls. She preferred diamonds, but the hat only came adorned with pearls.

"I am not brown nosing. I am just being socially polite as we negotiate the details of your new assignment. How do you like my new straw hat?" He asked pointing to his head and grinning. He was dressed in a summer, white silk suit with white shoes. The cheap straw hat with a black band definitely did not go with his otherwise designer look.

"Your hat looks like something some country hick on Earth would wear while driving a farm tractor. In my opinion, you are getting old, blind, and your taste in clothing is slipping." She stated pulling a fourteen inch long metal nail file from her pocket and started filing her perfectly manicured nails.

God removed the straw hat from his head for a moment and took a good look at it. Sometimes she annoyed him with her honesty and her mouth. However, she was the only angel that would look him in the eye and tell him what was what. He placed the Amish straw hat back on his head and was about to retort when Osceola beat him to it.

"You can't discipline me for telling you the truth." She stated in her sticky, syrupy, sweet female voice while making hideous sounds with her nail file. "Did Mrs. God choose that hick farmer hat for you?"

"Don't start in on Mrs. God, Osceola. You know she out dresses all of us and has better taste than you and I put together. She is my woman and I won't stand for you bad mouthing her in your devious way."

"Touchy this morning, aren't you. Did Mrs. God fail to make you your morning coffee?"

God bit his lip and decided not to get in a war of words with her. If he didn't need her so bad, he might just send her to Hell for a few days to think over her comments about Mrs. God. However, he had to do what was best for his Kingdom.

"Get used to cheap, hick farmer, straw hats like I have on and little, white caps with ribbons hanging down. I am sending you down on assignment to an Amish community in the Midwest region of the United States. I am relieving you of your death angel duties temporarily. You will be going down as a guardian angel and on a special mission. I have a shortage of guardians right now. Several are on holiday, some are on honeymoons, and several have just retired and have asked to be placed on cruise ships. I have this Amish guardian angel position open that I don't have anyone to fill. Until you assume your new Eastern Gate guard position, you will be filling in and looking out for some Amish women who are in danger for various reasons. The Devil has zoned in on their husbands turning them away from me and toward darkness."

"You want me to baby sit a group of gray dressed, white, starchy caps with ribbons? You have got to be kidding! I was a good old Baptist on Earth before my crossing, not a white cap. What do I know about plain Jane white caps? I was a designer dressed, sing in the choir, barbecued rib eating, stiletto Baptist. I was also the church's worst gossip who killed with my tongue. Have you seen those little wimpy women? They follow their husbands around when they are out in public and never open their mouths. Send someone else. I am a designer Baptist girl, not a voiceless white cap."

"I remember when, as a Baptist, you crossed over. I had a shortage of

Death Angels at the time. You and your deadly tongue were right for the job. Now, it is time for me to move you up the ladder. Helping the Amish women on this mission find their voices is fine with me. I happen to like sticky syrup or I would have sent you to Hell long ago."

"Now God, I am a shopping in Paris and designer label loving angel; not a needle, thread, and three yards of fabric one. However, you haven't sent me to Hell because you know I have a key to it."

"I give you credit for being the best dressed death angel in Heaven. Also, I will give you credit for having transported way more than your share of souls over. However, I am not giving you any choice. I need you to guard a settlement of white caps. You have the ability to do group guarding. You have proven that by the huge groups of souls you have carried over from Earth's disasters. Your three hundred and seventeen last year, at one time, was a record. The most any other death angel has transported over at one time is thirteen. You are good and you know it, a pro."

"I am good and you know it!" Osceola retorted in her syrupy, sticky voice as she reached up and snatched the straw hat off his head and walked away with it, twirling it on her nail file. She then tossed it away into the air and it disappeared. "I will pick you up a suitable white hat in Paris on my next mission. It takes a woman with taste to see that a man is dressed properly for his position in life. You are not a cheap straw hat man. You can tell Mrs. God I said so, if you want. Perhaps I could take her shopping and clue her in as to what a man in your position should be wearing."

"Don't start a cat fight with Mrs. God, Osceola. You will lose!" He stated crossing his fingers behind his back for lying. "Take this Amish position willingly and I might grant you leave to go north in the USA afterward to fish a couple of days with that long legged Jack Rabbit man that you are so fascinated with."

"You will grant me a couple days leave with my Jack Rabbit?" She asked in shock. He had previously told her that he had chosen an angel to pair her with after she assumed her Eastern Gate position. Her Jack Rabbit was no angel. He was rough around the edges and lived in a little fishing cabin on a lake in the north in the United States. If she popped in on him, he probably would smell like fish he had been cleaning or insect repellent. Also, he was sure to have on three day old dirty underwear and hadn't changed the sheets on his bed in a month. He was a rough around the edges man who needed a woman like her to tame him. The thought of his long legs and arms wrapped around her caused her to shiver. He probably even had a beard now. There was nothing pretentious about him and she was nuts about him. If she weren't an angel and could return to Earth, she would turn him into a good old Baptist boy who manned the barbecue grills and the fish fryers at church for Sunday dinners. She might like him smelling like barbecue sauce, hickory smoke, and catfish. He would be a Baptist Bible thumping, offering taking deacon in the church after she tamed him.

"I am in a pinch, Osceola. If you don't go, I will have to send one guardian angel for each of the Amish women and I am too short of help right now." He replied taking a comb from his pocket and running it thru his white hair. Her pulling his hat off had unexpectedly left his hair mussed. "Two fishing days with the Jack Rabbit is a very generous bonus on my part, considering I have someone in mind to mate you with."

"Damn it God, why me?" Osceola whined in her syrupy, sticky, sweet voice that was trying to catch one fly all dressed in white that was annoying her. "Jack is a bribe that you know I won't turn down."

God answered, "Watch your language and why not you? You are the best angel I have. Granted you are a death angel, but you are the best. Pack your flight bag and drop the sweet talk. It doesn't work with me. You leave tonight. On your way out of the garden, will you tell my dog walker to quiet those hounds of heaven she is walking! The barking is driving me crazy."

"Since when do you need a dog walker? Mrs. God usually does that. She loves your hounds."

"Since Frances Periwinkle arrived on Heaven's shore and has failed every angel assignment I have sent her on. She is a sweet, syrupy, sticky voiced girl just like you. However she is spastic and capable of spilling her glass of water with someone else holding it. Walking my dogs is all I can come up with for a vocation for her. To be honest, when I was watching her earlier, it was my dogs walking her. I don't know what I am going to do with her and she is full of herself to boot. She asked me to let her skip guardian angel school and be sent directly out on guardian missions because she did not need to be trained. Check her out on your way out of the garden. She will be carrying a pooper scooper."

"Is that how you felt about me, when I first arrived on Heaven's shore?" Osceola asked eyeing him and not smiling. She had done a couple weeks as a dog walker before being assigned to death angel duty.

"You are black skinned with black hair and she is white skinned with straight brown hair worn in a ponytail. If it wasn't for obvious differences in how the two of you culturally look, the two of you could be sisters or mother and daughter. She is full of herself and mouths me just like you. She even has your syrupy voice."

"If you are planning on replacing me with her, I am not going to be happy with you, White Suit. Don't you dare give her my death angel job. I don't want your promotion to the Eastern Gate or that angel you plan to mate me with. Your Frances Periwinkle is not getting my key to Hell either." Osceola stated loudly in her syrupy, sticky voice suddenly feeling threatened by a new arrival in Heaven whom he had said was just like her.

CHAPTER TWO

Call of The Morning Rain

Cold, spitting rain was pecking at the windows of the Toombs' farmhouse. The tin roof on the back porch was echoing the sounds of the raindrops hitting it. It was a pleasant sound announcing the ending of the sunny days of autumn. Thanksgiving was just a couple weeks ahead and cold weather was approaching. The farm's fall harvest had been abundant and now Naomi Toombs was ready to settle in for a pleasant November of quilting and making pumpkin and apple butter. She was seven months pregnant and very happy about the approaching birth of a daughter. She had seen an English doctor and got to see her unborn child on what looked like a television screen. It was a little sin of looking that she had indulged herself with. The Amish as a rule did not have their photos made due to preaching against graven images. Naomi was thrilled her baby was going to be a girl. She already had a boy, a five year old son named Adam. He was a papa's boy and trailed her husband Joel everywhere. Life was good and their crops had provided them with a nice little nest egg.

Naomi was busy at her wood cook stove when her husband Joel entered the kitchen looking a little edgy. She had two skillets on the stove, one for sausage and eggs and the other for a pan of cow's milk gravy. Homemade biscuits were in the oven and starting to give off the smell of warm bread. She pulled open the door of the wood stove oven and took a peek at the biscuits to see how they were browning. Every biscuit was Amish brown and perfect. Reaching a brief moment where she could leave her skillets, she turned to greet her husband of almost six years.

"Good morning, husband. Did you sleep well?" She asked grinning and pushing a loose wisp of hair back up under her white bonnet.

"Did I sleep well . . . ?" He asked in a slur heading for the back door to look out. Once there, he leaned against the door frame.

Adam their son ran up to his father and wrapped his arms around his legs with excitement. "It is raining. The fish will bite. May we go fishing papa?"

"Fishing . . . ?" Joel replied sounding a bit confused as he continued to stare out the door. "Not today, Adam. I must go to town to sell our crop."

Naomi's ears perked up. They had sold their crop the day before and they never went to town in the rain. Five year old Adam was a severe asthmatic and they always shielded him from any elements that might trigger an attack. Only her vigilance as a mother and dedication to prayer kept him well.

"I don't feel we should go to town, Joel." She replied to his statement as she turned eggs in the skillet. "Rain and Adam's Asthma don't get along. He night take a cold. Also, we sold our crop yesterday."

"Perhaps Uncle Amos will go with me!" He replied inappropriately. His Uncle Amos had died three years prior.

Naomi was alarmed but too busy to worry for the moment. She had skillets on a hot fire. "I would return to town with you and leave Adam with your mother, but my big belly gets in the way now. The rude English look at me and ask all kinds of personal questions about our unborn child! I would not ask them concerning their big bellies, yet they fall all over themselves to inspect mine. They are very rude!" She said removing eggs from her skillet onto a platter alongside some sausage. She was down to making the gravy. She paused after putting grease, flour, salt, and pepper in the skillet the basic ingredients for gravy. She had to step to the back porch where it was cool to get fresh cow's milk for the gravy. She had milked their cow an hour before. She had let Joel sleep because he was to help with a barn raising later, which was very strenuous.

"You are with child?" Joel asked seeming lost in whatever it was he was looking at out the back door.

Naomi shot him a glance but continued with her breakfast preparation by setting the table.

"Naomi . . . ," Joel called. "Who is the black woman out back staring at our door?" He asked pointing to the field.

Joel Toombs was about to walk away from his family and abandon them for good. He had wandered away on many occasions enjoying city life and then returning and pretending he had amnesia and did not know where he had been. He had run out of stories to tell to play mad and walk away. While sleeping in, he had come up with a new one. There were no black people in the vicinity of the Amish settlement. He would pretend he was seeing a black person calling him to meet them in his garden patch. Of course, Naomi would fall for it and think him mad once he told her the black person was wearing a summer dress, English spike heels, and was picking strawberries which were not in season in November.

Leaving her gravy making, Naomi walked over to her kitchen cabinets and took a quick peek out the window above them. She had to stretch to do so. Her belly was always in the way now. She saw no one.

"Where do you see a woman, Joel? I don't see anyone. Perhaps she wants to buy eggs or some of my pumpkin butter." She replied scanning the farm thru her kitchen widow. Rain was peppering against the window making it hard to see.

"She stands just to the right of the garden patch and has on a white summer like robe and is picking our strawberries." He stated straining and peering out the door as though he were trying to get a better view.

"Strawberries . . .?" Naomi questioned thinking he meant turnips or beets. He didn't reply, so she joined him at the door to try to see whom he was speaking of. She could not see anyone. Suddenly, she knew why her husband seemed odd this morning. Dropping her head and biting her lip, she closed her eyes and prayed silently. "Please God, not again!"

"I am going to go ask her why she is picking our strawberries." Joel stated taking his black Amish hat from a hook by the back door and putting it on his head.

"Wait, Joel! Go speak with her after breakfast. I am sure she will still be there. When we are thru eating, you can take her a biscuit and I will put straw-berry jam on it." She stated trying to distract him.

"No, I must go. I hear her calling me asking me to help her pick a bushel basket full." He replied cracking the screen door to exit.

"Joel, the black strawberry woman is not there. Her voice is in your head. You are seeing things again. You must fight this madness. Sit down at the table and have breakfast with your son. I will walk out to the garden patch with you after our meal. Let Adam, your son, eat first." She stated nervously trying to snag his attention.

"The woman in white beyond the garden bids me come and carry her bas-ket of berries. I must go!" He said fully opening the back screen door prepar-ing to step out. He let his hand slip down to his pocket to make sure he had his crop money.

Naomi grabbed Joel by the arm with one hand trying to prevent him from walking without a coat out into the morning rain which was now coming down in torrents. She did not know that he had hidden himself a jacket and other items in a black plastic bag behind a tree near the black top road behind their farm.

Joel roughly grabbed Naomi's hand and removed it from his arm. Then he grabbed and held both of her wrists to restrain her from holding on to him and glared into her eyes not saying a word. With one rough violent shove, he sent her sprawling onto the floor. She screamed in pain landing on her big pregnant belly. He then began kicking her.

Adam ran to his mother's side and jumped between her and his father who was about to kick her in the ribs.

"Papa, you will not kick mama again!" Five year old Adam yelled. "You shame me, papa!"

"Who are you?" Joel asked lowering his foot. "Are you a neighbor's boy?" he asked continuing his deception.

"He is your son, Joel!" Naomi yelled loudly thru tears, labor, and shooting pains all over from being kicked. "He is your son and I am Naomi your wife. Please help me! I am in trouble with the baby."

Joel ignored her. He had not wanted either of the children born to him and Naomi. They had been nooses around his neck holding him to the farm and a way of life he did not want. He turned towards the screen door and then exited grinning when his back was to her and Adam.

From the floor, unable to rise, Naomi yelled and begged for him to come back and help her. He ignored her and just walked away in to the rainy, November morning.

Seeing he was not returning, Naomi turned to her son. "Run, Adam, down the road and get your grandparents. Tell them your father has wandered off into the field again and I need help because the baby is coming. Wear your hat!"

"Yes, mama . . . !" Five year old Adam stated running for the front door of the farmhouse where his hat hung on a low peg that had been placed there just for him. Taking his hat from the peg, he put it on ignoring his coat hanging next to it, and exited the front door to run in the rain for a quarter of a mile to get help for his mother. Adam was barely five years old. Naomi and Joel had been married for going on six.

Naomi managed to get up in spite of her severe pain and stumble to the back door holding her belly with both hands. The action in her belly felt like the baby was shaking uncontrollably. She was sure the baby was having seizures. Tears streamed from her eyes as she realized her unborn baby had also been hurt in the fall and from Joel's kicking. There was nothing she could do to comfort or help her unborn child.

Looking out the back door, she tried to see which way Joel was headed so the brethren could follow him. She could not see him anywhere. Beyond their back field was a county black top road. If he made it there, he would once more disappear till his madness cleared.

A severe pain doubled Naomi over. She held to the door frame to keep from passing out. Her world was falling apart.

Naomi had hoped, after Joel's last episode of madness, that he was free of it. Two good years of calm had blessed them. Now his mental condition, his craziness was back. She wondered how long he would be gone this time. She couldn't run after him because she was in labor.

When Joel and Naomi were first married, he would wander off two and three days at a time always returning apologetic not knowing where he had been. Right before Adam turned three, he left crazy and didn't return for six months. Now, he was walking away in his madness again.

Fear gripped Naomi as her water broke. She was barely seven months pregnant. Then she passed out and lay unconscious on her kitchen floor by the door. She and her baby were in serious trouble.

Joel Toombs stood drenched from the rain behind a tree on the back of his twenty acre farm that his parents had given him and Naomi for a wedding present. Hurrying, he put on a set of English clothing and a rain slicker he had purchased on his trip to town the day before to sell his crop. He had hidden the items the day before behind the tree in a black plastic bag to protect them from the elements. He had pre-planned to walk away on the first rainy morning after he had his crop money. He knew Naomi would not send his sickly son running and following him in the rain, nor would she run after him being pregnant. His kicking her had not been part of the plan. It seemed all of his hatred for his parents and her gushed out suddenly and he released it knowing he was not returning. He should have slit his son's throat but he knew he could not get by with that. Law officers would chase him down and send him to prison for murder. He wanted a new life, not prison. If it hadn't been for self preservation, he would have gotten rid of the sickly child that Naomi had bore him. No man wanted a sissy son. Now, he had his crop money and he was free. He would assume a new identity and entice many women to crawl into his bed who knew what lovemaking was all about, his pleasure, not theirs. Naomi could die, sink, or swim. He didn't care which.

With his crop money now in his new jeans pocket, Joel knew he had to hurry and hitch a ride to freedom and his red head. He could hear his back porch emergency farm bell being rung repeatedly. The bell rope was probably being pulled by Naomi for men to come and chase after him. He had to make haste.

Pulling his new rain slicker on, he took one last fleeting glance at the twenty acre farm he hated. There was no explaining to his parents or Naomi that he did not want to be Amish. His marriage had been arranged by the brethren and Naomi came to him a fifteen year old Amish orphan from Pennsylvania. His parents forced him to marry her the day after she arrived on her sixteenth birthday. He never wanted to see her, the farm, the brethren, sickly Adam, or his parents ever again. They were not what he wanted out of life. A redhead he had met on one of his pretend madness wanderings was what he wanted along with secret others for sex. One woman just did not satisfy him.

It took about fifteen minutes for Adam to run to his grandparent's neighboring farm and bring his grandparents back. Seeing that his bloody, battered daughter-in-law was in serious trouble, Abraham Toombs immediately ran to the back porch and took over for Adam who was ringing the emergency bell for the brethren to come. He then ran for the nearest English neighbor and used their phone to call for an ambulance. He knew that if Naomi died, Joel would be charged with murder because his grandson had witnessed the kicking and abuse of Naomi.

That rainy, fall morning was a nightmare in Naomi Toombs secluded, Amish world. Her life began a slow crumble leaving her with little to hold on to. She was flown by helicopter to the nearest hospital where she was treated for life threatening injuries as well as was given a C-section to try to save her premature daughter. Mary, her injured baby lived fifteen minutes. Ten days later she returned home with empty arms, a broken rib, sprained ankle, broken wrist, and a black eye and other bruising that was slowly healing.

Martha Toombs, Naomi's mother-in-law, had kept Adam while she was in the hospital. Her mother-in-law had never particularly cared for her son saying he was undisciplined, pampered, and always got what he wanted. Naomi, unconscious when she was flown to the hospital, had no say in who was to care for Adam while she was gone. Martha Toombs took Adam home with her and did not pamper or carefully watch him. She put him out in the rain doing chores along with her husband and other son who was one year older than Joel. Adam took a cold which developed into Pneumonia and he was dead five days later. Martha Toombs had not sought medical help for him till it was too late.

Naomi's two children slept in wooden coffins in the Amish's private cemetery. The brethren had made the coffins. She had not been able to attend the funeral of either of her children and she had not gotten a chance to say goodbye or kiss Adam one last time as he slept in death. Both of her children were buried before she was dismissed from the hospital. There was no closure for her. Her final memories of her children were not good ones. She remembered her newborn baby girl gasping for breath as she lay dying in her arms and Adam watching as his father kicked her unmercifully.

Once Naomi was home from the hospital, Joel's mother, Martha, became a nightmare not wanting to admit her part in Adam's death. She was shocked when her mother-in-law approached the brethren and insisted that she had caused Joel's madness and had provoked him into the abusing of her in an effort to keep her son from being shunned for the violence. Naomi became an escape goat for Joel's mother who told everyone in the Amish community that God's wrath had taken Naomi's children because she had not been a proper wife to her son and also that she was a witch. Her mother-in-law Martha was ruthless in the vicious gossip she spread and none of it true.

Murder is murder no matter what form it takes. In the case of Adam, Martha had let him die without medical attention. Joel killed his unborn child by injuring her in the womb.

Martha Toombs was mad, just as her son pretended to be. Hiding her own guilt of not caring for her grandson, she told anyone that would listen that Naomi was stirring a black pot of milk weed poison on the morning her son had walked away and had used it to cast a spell on Joel causing him to see things and go crazy. The so called witch's pot of milk weed poison was an unfinished pan of milk gravy that Naomi had been making to go on their biscuits for breakfast. Martha in her madness insisted Naomi be shunned on the grounds that she was a witch who had caused the craziness of her son and the deaths of her two children.

Naomi, sick with grief, stayed to her-self as Martha viciously maligned her. In her heart, she knew that she had tried to prevent Joel from walking away in his crazy state. Her conscious was clear and she also knew that she had been the best wife and mother that she knew how to be. It was Joel that had done the violent pushing, kicking, and the walking away from his family. She was not guilty and if she had not been in the hospital, she would have seen that Adam received medical care and he would be alive.

After the nightmare of the event had distanced itself, Naomi waited in the big lonely farmhouse for Joel to return, hoping it would just be a few days or a few weeks till he came wandering back, apologizing, and clearing her name. To her dismay, he never returned home to vindicate her reputation and admit to his part in the fateful morning's events. Her Amish community ended up shunning her at Martha's insistence, on the grounds that she was a witch.

After the shunning, Naomi's only visitor came in the form of an occasional knock on her front door by her father-in-law Abraham Toombs who asked if she had heard from Joel. He seemed to want to tell her something, but could not find the words to do so. After asking, he would quickly leave not wanting to be seen at her front door by his wife Martha. Once he spoke words to her that she did not fully understand.

"I will make Joel seek medical help for his inherited madness, when he returns. I know you were making gravy the morning he walked away and I am fed up with Martha's gossip and her witch story. She is the witch, not you. I have put up with years of disrespect from Martha because of my wedding vows. I am sorry, Naomi, but there is nothing I can do till Joel returns. Check your back porch every morning. I will leave food items for you there before I start my milking. Please do not tell anyone that I have been here or about the food items. Martha is crazy enough to accuse me of adultery with you. This Amish community is my life and I have never kicked anyone or broken my wedding vows. You and I are unfortunate victims of a devil woman. I am bound to her and you are lashed by her tongue. Survive, Naomi, and one day see Martha and Joel get what is coming to them."

CHAPTER THREE

Walking Away

Time did not heal Naomi Toombs' heart or make her forget the nightmare day that took all of her family from her. The nightmare seemed never ending and dragged on for years. Each fall triggered an onset of bad memories and then depression set in for the winter. It had been five years since Joel had walked away into the rain. He had not returned. Naomi knew she could not mentally handle another long winter of depression. Five years of waiting for Joel to return and her endless grief over her children's deaths was taking a toll on her. She had to get hold of herself and make new choices for her life. She had decided to say goodbye to her life that once was.

Walking down the dirt road in front of her property, she headed for the small Amish cemetery at the fork in the road to tell her children goodbye. Today was the end of her five year nightmare. She was leaving the Amish community. They did not want her. Joel had never returned to vindicate her and she was branded as a witch. None of the people she once knew and loved would associate with her. Joel had stolen her children from her and Martha had stolen her Amish life. It was time to tell her children goodbye and walk away.

An individual walked with Naomi, but she did not see the being. A huge black skinned woman wearing a white pantsuit and a gaudy gold head wrap walked beside her. It was Osceola Black Lightning, the death angel. She had transported the two souls of Naomi's children to the other side five years prior. Now she was on a temporary mission keeping an eye on the women of

Naomi's Amish settlement. God had bribed her into taking the position. Her mission was not to interfere in Naomi's life, but to be there should the devil in human flesh, named Joel, once more call on her. Osceola Black Lightning was a guardian who had been sent by God after Joel succumbed to darkness. On this particular morning, Osceola walked along on the dirt road in her gold stilettos accompanying Naomi, as any guardian would.

Turning into the cemetery, Naomi took a deep breath. Five years of grief and living alone had taken a toll on her. Reaching her children's graves, she pulled the grass that had grown up around the two huge common field rocks that she had placed on her children's graves for headstones. When Joel had walked away, he had all of their money from the crops in his pocket. All she had was about twelve dollars in a fruit jar that she had been saving to purchase material for a quilt. Joel had left her penniless. It had been a source of great stress that she had not been able to provide her children with proper headstones. She had barely kept herself fed with no one in the Amish community to help her, having been shunned. She now had to enter the land of the English and find work. There was no other choice. She could not sell the farm because Joel was not dead. However, she had slowly sold off all of the livestock, tools, and other personal possessions to feed her-self. Now, she had to walk away. She could no longer wait for Joel to return. She was sure that he had to be dead in a gutter somewhere or he would have returned to Adam his son. Her son was a papa's boy, although he had stood up for her when Joel had her on the floor kicking her.

Standing to take one last look at the graves, she wondered if Joel had ever loved her. She was sure that if she was the crazy one, she would not have pushed him down or abandoned him and Adam. Five years of waiting had taken its toll on her young love for Joel. She was not sixteen anymore and she wasn't sure whether she would welcome him back after all the misery he had caused her with his absence. She definitely would not subject another child to his abandonment of them. No longer a naïve, young bride; maturing Naomi was ready to abandon him and their marriage which was non- existent. She was ready to walk away and start over.

"I am sorry, Adam. I should not have sent you for your grandparents. We should have just let your father wander off and your baby sister die at home. I am sorry that your grandmother Martha chose to ignore your symptoms and let you die. She will pay in the judgment as she has made me pay for her sin here. Your father's madness was his sin, not ours. We have paid with great pain and sorrow and the giving of lives." Naomi stated unable to hold back a flood gate of tears. "I am tired of being alone, Adam. It has been five years and your father has not returned. Everyone has shunned me and I cannot attend church. Our house is empty and like a prison. I made my last flour into three biscuits this morning. There is nothing left to sell to feed and clothe me thru the winter. I cannot sell the farm. All I can do is just walk away. I haven't family to go home to, so I must go make a life for myself in the land of the English. I will find work there and start over. Sleep peacefully till I return and move your body to a land where we are loved."

Stooping down, she placed her hand over her heart and then touched her baby Mary's tiny grave. Closing her eyes, she shed her last tears. After a few moments, she opened her teary eyes and stood.

"Mary, I will always treasure the short time you rested in my arms and belly. I love you!"

Turning to Adam's grave, she continued, "I am leaving the farm in the hands of your Uncle James, your father's older brother. Perhaps, one day your father will return if he isn't dead. I plan to create a sane life for myself amongst the English. I will wait for your father no more. Five years is enough. The two of you take care of each other as you sleep awaiting the resurrection or my return to move your bodies to a new land of joy."

Naomi Toombs shed her last tears as she said her good-byes to her deceased children with a huge, black, female angel standing beside her. The invisible death angel cried with her. Naomi thought the drops of water, falling on her children's graves, were spitting rain. Angel's tears fall like rain cursing and blessing. The tears falling on Adam and Mary's grave were promises from Osceola Black Lightning that she would avenge their deaths. Osceola was a softie sometimes, but not often.

Guarding Naomi was Osceola Black Lightning's first duty on her new mission. She had just entered the Earth Realm a few moments before Naomi began her good byes to her children. She was a reaper of souls dark and light. She escorted them to the Judgment seat of God and then delivered the dark to Hell where she unlocked its gate for them. As a guardian angel, she hadn't proven herself yet. Standing and listening to the white cap cry and tell her children goodbye, touched her. She wept death angel rain and promises for vengeance. Then she dried her eyes on a designer hankie from Paris and pulled out a long metal nail file from her handbag to work on her nails while she waited on the white cap.

With her good byes said, Naomi returned to the farmhouse. There she packed a carry tote with one change of clothes, a comb, her scissors, needles, thimble case and a starter for sour dough bread in a half pint fruit jar. Last to go in was her Bible. She could only take what she could carry. She then put on all the clothes that she could possibly wear and still walk comfortably. Over that she wore her heavy winter cloak which she would use as a blanket at night. She would sleep wherever God provided her a place to lay her head.

Packed and ready to go, she pulled her wedding quilt from her bed and stuffed it into the wood stove and set it afire. Then she watched it and her Amish hopes and dreams burn. She had spent many hours in her teen year's hand quilting the treasured bedcover. Now, it represented the ending of her years of horror with a mad man and her marriage which she was laying down. Her wedding quilt and vows had not brought her happiness.

Marriage to Joel had been a repetitive nightmare of him coming and going with no warning. She decided as she watched the quilt burn, she would never remarry. Her new life would be hers and she would create one in which she was not sitting in limbo waiting for a man to come home and literally going hungry. Martha had put a stop to Abraham bringing her food and staples to cook with. She had followed him one morning. She knew she must now put herself first and create a life in which she could live with or without a man in it and still eat, have a life, and not be shunned by others. She would head her new home when she created it.

The quilt disappeared in the flames. Naomi closed the wood stove's door and with it the one to her non-existent marriage. She had decided to declare Joel dead in the courts of the English so she could move forward. Whether he was alive or dead, she would be free of him. Also, she had decided within herself that God did not join light and dark, man did. Her Bible said to flee darkness. Joel was dark with his madness, abandonment of her, and the murder of her two children. She would let darkness go and live in the light of a future better choice.

Walking out her front door with almost nothing but the clothes on her back, Naomi closed the door to her Amish world and its nightmares. Looking to the sky, she watched one huge rain cloud drift away overhead peppering the farm's landscape with raindrops. After that, the sky turned to sunshine. "That is odd!" She muttered to herself. "One cloud and it spits rain on this and Joel's parents' farm only. What is that a sign of?"

Naomi Toombs felt like she was a hundred and two. Life and her Amish community had not been kind to her. She had reached a personal life crossroad. Feeling a hundred and two, she had made a new choice to be reborn.

In the five previous years, she had two visitors from her Amish community of brethren. Because of Martha's mad act of getting her shunned as a witch, no one had been willing to share a meal with her or converse with her, much less share her sorrow and comfort her. The English mailman had been her only steady contact with the human race. She made a point of being at the box to take her mail from him each day. He had been her only friend and he probably did not know it.

Naomi took a huge breath to clear her head of the past. Then she took another in preparation to enter the scary land of the English ahead. She would need to face her fears of the heathen who lived there. She had to work and make her way in their world and that meant interacting with them. She could no longer avoid them because they were rude or didn't embrace her values. She had to live in their world, no choice in the matter. That meant she must smile, work beside them, and take their money for her breads when she got her baking business started. One day, she would write Father Abraham and thank him for what he did do for her and ask him if he would like to come in his old age and live with her in the land of the English. Somehow, she felt that he was a very unhappy man in his vows with Martha. Perhaps one day he would need to walk away also. She would send the letter to the postman and ask him to give it to Abraham and Abraham only. She knew all Hell would break loose if Martha got a hold of the letter. Martha was not included in her invitation.

CHAPTER FOUR

Molly's Many Husbands

Pulling her gray cloak about her for protection, Naomi took a deep breath and increased the speed of her walking. She had chosen to walk away from her Amish settlement early while the brethren were in their barns milking and doing chores. She was not in the mood to have them stare or whisper, "There goes the witch." Plus, she did not want the embarrassment of none on the road offering her a ride in their buggies. She had decided to walk away early and in peace. As she did so, she prayed for divine guidance.

"Please, God, help me find peace for my weary soul amongst the English, as well as work. Guide me to my highest good and a life that is right for me. I am asking you to help me put darkness, Joel, and my marriage behind me. I no longer desire to be linked to darkness. I know now that there is a Devil and he is a spirit that travels in human form. I am fleeing him and a female Devil traveling in the human body form known as my mother-in-law. I now understand that Satan walks in human flesh and not in a far off pit somewhere. Help me to stay clear of walking devils. Send me, on my journey, angels of light traveling in human flesh."

Osceola Black Lightning had changed from the clothes she had worn at the cemetery. She was in the backwoods now walking behind Naomi. Camouflage hunter's pants, jacket, and hat were more appropriate and that is what she had on, except that she had forgot to change her shiny gold stilettos. As she walked, she read all of Naomi's thoughts and got a little teed at Martha

Toombs for her disrespect of calling Naomi a witch. Letting Naomi get a head of her, she suddenly grinned. Then, disappearing like a flash of lightning, she returned to the Amish community and the kitchen of Martha Toombs. The woman wasn't up cooking breakfast for her husband. She was still in bed and Abraham was going out the back door eating a dry piece of bread with peanut butter on it. That further teed Osceola. Abraham was a good man.

Removing her nail file from her hunter's jacket and grinning like the cat that ate the canary, Osceola gave a little swish and sway with her file and on Martha's kitchen wood stove set a huge black witch's cauldron filled with milk weed and frogs from the Egyptian Nile. Then she swayed and swished the nail file again and two ladies from the Amish settlement stood at her back door knocking and wondering why they were on Martha's porch before breakfast. She then pointed the nail file at the back door and it opened on its own as she swished it and swayed it again and Martha stood shaking her head having been awakened from her sleep to find out she was standing in her nightgown in front of her wood stove and she had her kitchen broom in her hand.

"I must be sleep walking," Martha muttered and then spotted the huge cauldron of frogs and milkweed on her stove and then heard behind her foot-steps entering her kitchen. She turned to see two of the elder's wives with vis-ible shock on their faces staring at her.

"She cast a spell on us." One managed to say. "I was in my kitchen cooking oatmeal and now I am here."

Then both of the elder's wives backed out Martha's kitchen door and then ran across the fields in fright returning to their homes.

Osceola was pleased. God always said an eye for an eye and a tooth for a tooth. Martha had called Naomi a witch. Now she would be called one. Then she swished and swayed her nail file and the cauldron disappeared with Martha watching. Martha then ran out of her back door yelling and screaming that she had been cursed by a witch. They couldn't blame Naomi. She was not there. Osceola was sure that it was going to be a very interesting day in the Amish settlement with juicy hot gossip. Gossip was all the white caps had for entertainment. They had no flat screens. She thought about putting gates to hell on the front of all the outhouses for the men in retaliation, but had sec-ond thoughts. God would really get her if one of her white caps accidentally entered one of her outhouse Hell doors and got a little sunburned.

"An eye for an eye and a tooth for a tooth . . .!" Osceola yelled in a thunderous sticky, syrupy, voice that made all the other guardian angels in Heaven turn and take notice. She was good.

A couple of hours passed and Naomi, unaware she had an angel accompanying her, arrived at a bridge spanning Sac Creek, a few miles out of Pleasant Hope, Missouri. Stopping to rest, she leaned on the bridge railing eyeing the lazy waters below flowing gently to nowhere. Scanning the wild vines and grasses on the banks leading sharply down to the creek, she spotted a Cottonmouth snake sunning itself on a rock. The serpent seemed oblivious to her presence. It seemed content to doze in the sun, probably its last chance before hibernating. Missouri weather could be sunny and warm one day and snowing the next. Like the snake, she now had to find a rock somewhere to hibernate beneath for the winter.

"Goodbye, Mr. Snake stated Naomi. I must continue my journey now. May you have a pleasant fall and winter in your home beneath your rock. I go to find a pleasant rock of my own in the city somewhere."

As she turned from the railing, an old, faded, yellow station wagon pulled alongside her and stopped. The elderly woman driver rolled her window down.

"I am heading up to highway 13 and the gas station. Would you like a lift?" The white headed, weather beaten, flannel dressed older woman asked.

"Yes, I would appreciate a ride. Thank you!" Naomi said and then walked around the car and got in the front seat after placing her carry tote in the car's back floorboard.

"I was so glad to see you standing there at the bridge. I need another woman to vent to this morning. My husband is grating on my last nerve!" The lady driver stated and then introduced herself. "I am Molly Cameron."

"I am Naomi Toombs and I also would enjoy some woman talk. It has been a long while for me."

"Where are you headed, Naomi?"

"I will travel as far as my legs will carry me. Whenever they give out, I will be home."

"I got in this old wagon once a few years back and drove till I ran out of gas. I didn't care where I was going just as long as I didn't have to go back and look at my husband. It was just one of those days when I felt I needed space and didn't need him. It was a dumping day for me."

"I understand. Today is my dumping day. I will walk till I run out of gas." Naomi replied with a slight smile on her face.

"Are you running away from a man or just life in general?" Molly asked slowing her car to let at least ten dogs get out of the road. They looked like coon hounds and they were everywhere on the blacktop making the road impassable. A huge black woman dressed in camouflage stood on the shoulder of the road whistling for the dogs to come to her.

"My life for the last few years has been a nightmare and not of my choosing. Like your feelings when you sped away in your yellow station wagon, I do not care where I am going; I just know that I am going."

Molly slowed and rolled down her window to speak with the huge black woman in camouflage.

"Those are some fine coon hounds. Have you been lucky this morning on your hunt?"

"Honey . . ." The huge black woman began in a sticky, syrupy, sweet voice. "These aren't coon hounds. They are Hounds of Heaven. I spotted them a few moments ago. They got loose from God's dog walker. I am doing a little brown nosing by retrieving them. They are demon sniffing dogs."

"Bring them over to my place later and let them take a whiff of my current husband. There isn't a doubt in my mind that he isn't the laziest, beer drinking, devil that ever walked the face of this Earth. Just open my front door and turn them loose on him."

Osceola Black Lightning snickered. "You can see me?"

"Yep, and those are some gold shoes you have on. Don't you think black hunting boots would make more sense to wear with what you have on?"

About that time, one of the hounds of Heaven decided to use Osceola's leg for a water hydrant. She squealed and jumped back. It was too late. Her bare toes and her gold stilettos were dripping in dog urine.

Osceola looked down at her feet in disgust. "God now owes me one pedicure and a new pair of 14 Karat Gold spikes. Maybe I will put a lien on his hounds of Heaven till he pays up."

"You can tie your lost dogs in my barn if you want. You say a Mr. God owns them?"

"Yes and there is probably a reward out for them."

"Does Mr. God live around here?" Molly asked resting her left arm with her elbow out the driver's window.

"He lives in the big white house."

"I don't guess I know him." Molly then replied.

"You don't know God? Well if this good old choir singing, barbecued rib eating, Bible thumping, Baptist girl had the time, she would introduce you to him. However, I have got to get these dogs home. If you see a little thirteen year old four eyed girl with a pony tail along the road, tell her I caught her dogs and she is out of a dog walking job."

"I will do that."

Molly rolled up her window and crept forward in her vehicle past the dogs, returning her attention to Naomi.

"My second husband was a terror. He complained about my cleaning, my housekeeping, my too big of a butt, my hair do, my makeup, or lack of it, my spending, and everything in general. I am a patient woman and I put up with a lot. However, I don't do crazy. One morning I had a headache. I was really too ill to be up cooking his breakfast. However, I was committed to my marriage and my routine. I got out of bed with the worst, damn, throbbing migraine I have ever had. I made him breakfast and packed his lunch. When he came to the breakfast table and sat down, I was just pulling a pan of biscuits from the oven. I had left them in a little too long due to my headache. Anyway, he looked at me and asked me why I was a dumb ass who always burnt the biscuits. That was the breaking point. I flipped that pan of biscuits hot from the oven over and let them all fall into the middle of the kitchen floor and stormed out. I drove till I had no gas or headache. I ended way up north of Kansas City at a truck stop when my legs, my car's gas, wore out."

"I too have burnt biscuits. However, my Joel actually liked them that way. He said they were good coffee dunkers." Naomi replied snickering. "It is other craziness that I am running from."

"The only thing that got dunked at my house was the husband who called me a dumb ass. I dunked him in divorce court and left him there floating in his coffee cup of alimony." Molly replied joining her new woman friend in girl laughter.

"How did you get home from Kansas City? That is far away from here." Naomi asked wanting to hear the ending of the story.

"I held up a paper sign at the truck stop saying I was stranded, available, and wanted a ride. A truck driver from Springfield bought me some gas and followed me back home in his rig. He took advantage of my being stranded, available, and wanting a ride if you get my drift. I married him the day my divorce came thru. He became husband number three."

"You English marry and divorce so easy. The Amish do not divorce at all except for the sin of adultery."

"Divorcing my first husband was hard. I actually loved him. We had three children in their teens when I threw him out. I was working at a chicken processing plant in Springfield to bring in some extra money. Raising three teens wasn't cheap. I returned home one day early because the factory was temporarily between contracts and the work played out for the day. I found husband number one in my bed, on my sheets, with a nude woman who was not as pretty as me. That was hard. You put all your trust and faith in the first one. He is your knight in shining armor. I found him very hard to get over."

"Did you know the nude woman who was in your bed with your husband?" Naomi asked with big eyes.

"She was an Amish woman who lived a couple of miles or so from us at the time."

"An Amish woman committed adultery with your husband?" Naomi asked in shock. "We Amish, as a rule, are married for life. Your story surprises me greatly. Adultery is rare in our settlement and divorce never."

"I had no intention of getting a divorce or letting her and him get by with disrespecting me. I grabbed a pistol from the purse on my arm and put a bullet hole thru my bedroom ceiling and then shot between my husband's legs as he ran nude for his pickup truck. Then I went back to the bedroom and caught the woman in gray half dressed in just her bra and underwear trying to crawl out my window. She had ruined my new screen by pushing it out with a lamp. Boy was I mad."

"Did you shoot at her too?" Naomi asked totally into the wild story.

"Nope, I made her walk barefoot and half naked back to her farm across the fields in ninety-three degree hot afternoon sunshine. The two mile walk burnt her like a red tomato. I marched her up to her Amish husband holding my revolver on her and told him where I found her and that if he didn't believe me return to my farmhouse and look because her black stockings, shoes, and hair pins were still scattered on my sheets and floor."

"Did he go with you to look?"

"Oh yea, the dumb ass man followed me back two miles across the fields and took a look. He threw his straw hat down on the floor of my bedroom and mumbled something in German that I was sure was curse words."

"He said the no-no German curse words?" Naomi asked. "He must have been extremely angry. Did he gather up her things?"

"No, I think they are still in my attic somewhere. However, we got to consoling each other and he came to my house for supper for about six months. He was one great lover. I don't know what she saw in my two minute Charlie."

"What was your Amish lover's name?" Naomi asked totally intrigued by the sinful story that was breaking all of the Commandments.

"Abraham was his name and he was one good looking red headed man. His hair got all frizzy and he looked like a wild man when he was wet with sweat and we were making love. His hair had a mind of its own."

"Abraham is a common name among the Amish."

"It has been somewhere around twenty-seven going on twenty-eight years since I had the love affair with the Amish man and I walked his wife home at gun point."

"What was the woman's name?" Naomi asked innocently.

"Her name was Martha. She was odd like she had a screw loose."

"Her name was Martha and his name was Abraham!" Naomi stated repeating the names. Martha was a common Amish name amongst the women of her settlement. She tried to think of who amongst the brethren had wild red hair and then she bit her lip. Her father in law was white headed now. However, when she had married Joel ten years earlier, her father-in-law had wild, fly away, frizzy, red hair. Was Molly the reason Abraham was unhappy? Was her nightmare mother-in-law the nude woman with the sunburn? She snickered and knew that she should not be thinking about such things. She definitely did not want to think about her father-in-law being a great lover. That was sinful.

"Did the Amish man divorce his wife?" Naomi asked still fishing for details.

"No, he is still with her. As you said, Amish marry for life!"

"Do you ever see him?"

"Sometimes he winks at me, if we happen to end up in a public place together when no one is looking. However, we both knew way back then that there was no future in our seeing each other. He was married for life. We had one hot and heavy romance that year. I can still feel the tickle of his beard. It was red. I never liked red hair till I met him."

"Did he have another name besides Abraham?"

"I think I remember his middle name was Joel, or was it John? I have had a lot of lovers since him and middle names sort of get lost and muddled in your thinking."

"I think I have heard the older women of my community whisper of such a scandal. We do not speak publicly of such things. However, I heard one say to another in a whisper and then snicker, do not wander too far, you might come home with a sun burn, two bullets, and a black haired baby you can't explain to your red headed husband."

Molly laughed. "The stork was flying that year. I recall having a red headed baby I couldn't explain."

"I had no idea what the old women were whispering and joking about till now. I think I know your red headed Abraham. He is a good, kind, decent man even if he did commit adultery with you."

"Well, we both got our point across." Molly replied letting out a thunderous laugh for an older woman. "I believe God says an eye for an eye. She got a black haired baby to remember a man that ran from her when the chips were down. I got a red headed baby from her husband getting even with her."

"I thought the story was an old wives tale told to scare us younger women about the consequences of adultery."

"What is you father-in-law's name?" Molly asked lighting a cigarette.

"Abraham Toombs."

"Oh . . . !" Molly retorted grinning.

"Are your children by your first husband all doing well?" Naomi asked changing the subject.

"Yea, they are all grown and gone. I also have a niece named Karen that I have raised. She is about your age and lives in Paducah, Kentucky. She is a red head like my Amish lover. You would almost think she was mine."

"I understand!" Naomi giggled. "She is a very close niece."

"You have the picture, girl. I wasn't about to let any Amish man and his sunburned wife lay claim to her. She is my favorite child, although she calls me Aunt Molly."

Naomi thought about her white haired father-in-law, Abraham. He was a wonderful man, but Martha didn't sleep with him. They had separate bedrooms and only had two children, Joel and James their oldest son.

"Are you married till death?" Molly asked.

"My heart is dead. My marriage is dead. My husband went mentally crazy and no longer lives under the same roof as I. My English postman describes his mental disease using the term Schizophrenic. He hears voices."

"Would you like to talk about it? Sometimes it is easier to talk to a stranger."

"My husband has a mental madness and in the beginning of our marriage, he would disappear from our home two or three days at a time. The days progressed to weeks and then months. I don't know where he went or understood his saying he could not remember where he had been." Naomi replied.

"I had one of those disappearing acts. When he was home, lady voices would call on the phone pretending they were customers of his. He was an insurance man. I took out a big policy on him. I figured some woman's husband somewhere would kill that sucker off and make me a rich woman."

Naomi snickered. "What happened to that husband? Did you collect your insurance policy?"

"Damn right I did. One night, an irate jealous husband ran him off the road. His car kissed a tree killing him and his married lover. I bought myself this car with the money from the policy. I think I came out okay on that one. This old wagon has been a good one. I also paid off my farm and put Karen thru college with the insurance money."

"Are you married now?" Naomi asked loving the old woman's stories.

"I like a man in my bed on a cold night. Winter is just around the corner. I am a skinny old broad and I like a warm backside to put my feet against." She replied turning onto another black top road. "How about you, do you plan on getting a new foot warmer when you get to where-ever it is you are going?"

Naomi snickered. "I have never thought of a man as such. However, my feet have been cold for many nights while I have waited for my husband to return to me. I do miss the warmth of his body next to me."

"Well, I am thinking about dumping my current foot warmer. He is too lazy to mow the grass and we have a riding lawn mower. I was out in the spitting rain this morning doing some end of the growing season mowing. He didn't once come out and offer to help! He is a couch potato who watches TV all day. When I ran out of gasoline for the mower, I couldn't get him to run to the station to get me some. So, here I am telling you about it and going for mower gas." Molly stated. "Do you want to tell me about your children or do you have any?"

"I lost a baby girl when I was seven months pregnant. She lived fifteen minutes in my arms. My other child, a boy, caught pneumonia the same week and died. I buried both of my children in one week. Plus, my husband walked away hearing voices and was not there to share my grief. I have not seen my husband since then. He disappeared five years ago. The postman says he has probably died a street person in a city gutter somewhere."

"I am so sorry, sweetie! Do you have somewhere to go?"

"I will walk till my legs will not carry me any further. Then I will start over and live a life among strangers and try to forget my nightmare marriage and the unnecessary deaths of my children."

"Won't your husband come looking for you when he gets his head on straight?"

"I am tired of waiting. Also, I am not the sixteen year old girl who was once in love with him. I have decided to create a life without him. When he left, he kicked me as I lay on the floor in labor after he pushed me down. He kicked my belly repeatedly causing the death of a baby girl I carried. I will not put myself in that position again. It has taken me five years and much sorrow to lay down my Amish beliefs about marriage being forever. Forever for me ended with the death of my children. I waited for him to return, but not for the resuming of our marriage. I want to divorce him on the grounds of adultery. He brought a male disease home to me several years ago that he could have only gotten from sleeping with a harlot. I have the paperwork. I have the right to a divorce. When I was young, I was too frightened to leave him and go out on my own. That is no longer the case. I will live in the land of the English, sue him for a divorce if he is alive, and if possible have him charged with the murders of my children."

"I shot a bastard husband once who had been beating me."

"Did you kill him?" Naomi asked once more big eyed.

"My aim wasn't very good due to my not having my glasses on. I shot for his heart and put one bullet right thru his man thing. He died two weeks later. It was a good day!" She replied rolling down her window to flip out a cigarette butt. "I made a girl of him. He took a bottle of sleeping pills and died from them."

"You shot his man thing off?" Naomi asked in a shocked voice.

"I sure did. Afterward, he could not face that he had become a woman and that his years of being a Tom cat were over." Molly stated nonchalantly.

"Did you cry at his funeral?"

"I was in jail. His funeral was held without me." She replied lighting another cigarette. "I got six months in the county jail for relieving him of his manhood. I was too busy out on the side of the highway with the other jail birds in orange vests picking up litter to think of him. Plus the jail guard with the shot gun wasn't too bad to look at. I lost a husband but had a date with the guard when my six months was up."

"You are wonderful, Molly. I am so glad that I have met you. I have needed a woman to talk to who understands. My Amish sisters shunned me saying I had caused my husband's madness and it was God's wrath on me killing my children."

"Men think with their long john and can be absolute ass holes to women who truly care about them. Unlike most women, I am willing to be vocal and talk about it." She replied turning off on a country lane leading to a small cemetery deep in the woods. "Let me show you where my number four and five husbands sleep."

Molly drove her auto down a narrow grass covered road in the cemetery and pointed from the car window to two gravestones side by side. "That is them."

"Will you be buried next to them?" Asked Naomi looking.

"Hell no . . . !" She stated in a loud firm voice. "See that monster, tall, red rock over in the good side of the cemetery? That is where I will be put. I worked and paid for that red granite monster and I am not sharing it with any ass hole husband. When I rest in peace, it will be in a silk lined coffin, beneath an expensive stone, and with no man telling me to get up, and put the coffee on. I will have a thermos of coffee from the local restaurant buried with me."

Naomi broke out in belly laughter. After calming herself, she replied, "I will give all your words some serious consideration when I reach my peaceful somewhere destination. Perhaps, I will not rise early and make coffee and biscuit dunkers for any man ever again. I like the idea of having a thermos of coffee buried with me."

Molly drove out of the cemetery and returned up a lane to the black top.

"Would you like to tell me about your husband's disease he brought home to you? I bet you have not told anyone but me. Burdens are easier if someone helps carry them!"

"I was with child when Joel started his wandering off to town for two or three days at a time. Returning home, he would claim not to know where he was. When my son was just a month old, he wandered off and didn't return for six months. I forgave him because his mother insisted he was somehow going crazy. After the six month episode, he became very ill with his man thing in pain. I accompanied him to town to an English doctor to get it cured. The doctor took me aside and told me my husband had got a sex disease from sleeping possibly with a prostitute. Joel had to take medicine and so did I because he had slept with me. I thought about cutting his manhood off with my butcher knife. He had defiled me and I was too ashamed to ever tell anyone about it. I was angry and my vow of non-violence was in serious jeopardy. I took my butcher knife and threw it far under the floor of the house till I raged no more. Finally, I swallowed my pride knowing that he was my husband for life and if I wanted children, I had to forgive him."

"It is always the woman that is expected to do the forgiving and the putting up with. I bet he didn't once apologize to you did he?"

"He claimed to not remember what he did in the English world. The wanderings continued for a day here and a day there and then we hit a good spell and his madness went away for two years. We had two wonderful years together and I conceived our second child, Mary. Then my two years of happiness ended. One rainy morning he woke up crazy, pushed me into the floor causing my seven month pregnancy to end and my baby to be born early and live only fifteen minutes. My son who was asthmatic ran for help and died from pneumonia. It was raining hard the day he went for help. My husband left me to bleed out on the kitchen floor and walked across our field and has never returned. For five years I have sat in a lonely farmhouse waiting for justice. It did not come. I have laid my old life down and do not intend to return to it. Some day, I will send for the remains of my children and move them to where ever I end up."

"You and I, Naomi, have been walked on by men who promised to love and protect us forever. As mature women, we know that we must love ourselves, provide for ourselves, and create worlds to live in that cannot be taken from us by any ass hole coming or going."

"You are right, Molly. It is time for me to love myself and move forward into a new life, one that I have created and do not have to flee. I will never naively love and trust a man again. If a man wants to be with me, he will come live in my world, not me his."

"The thing to remember, Naomi, is to become all you can be and never depend on a man for finances. If you can take care of yourself, you can exist with or without a man. You are somebody and will always be somebody. For instance, a woman marries a doctor and devotes her life to him and becomes known as the doctor's wife with no identity of her own. Should the good doctor dump her, running off with his nurse, she suddenly does not know who she is because she is no longer the doctor's wife. If that woman had pursued her own career as a doctor, lawyer, teacher, etc, his dumping her might hurt, but it would not leave her without an identity. Keep your own identity, Naomi. Never latch on to a man's. That is a going nowhere ride."

"I guarantee you, Molly, I will be somebody! Mrs. Joel Toombs is history. I plan to become Naomi the owner of a bread baking and jelly business. Perhaps I will be known as Naomi, the Amish Bread Baker."

"I am Molly the Gun Smith. I have sort of developed a passion for shot guns and revolvers over the years and have turned it into a business."

"You are wonderful, Molly. I wish I had known you the last five, lonely years. We could have shared many hours having woman talk."

"Well, we have met now. That is how life has intended it. We can keep in touch by mail and you will have me to come home to, should you ever decide to do so. I will always have a spare room made up and waiting for you, even if it is just for a weekend visit. I just might teach you to shoot a revolver. It might come in handy some day." Molly stated pulling to a stop on the blacktop where it intersected highway thirteen.

"Thank you for stopping and giving me a ride. I desperately needed someone to talk to this morning."

"Become Naomi the baker who spreads her home floor with men as rugs. Walk on them but never let them walk on you from this day forward." Molly stated digging in her purse for a scrap of paper and a pen. Then she wrote two addresses on it and handed the paper to Naomi saying, "The first address is mine. The second is that special niece of mine who lives in Paducah, Kentucky. Should you wander that way, she has an apartment house. I think the two of you could become good friends."

"Thank you, Molly." Naomi stated tucking the addresses away in her dress pocket. "What will you do about your couch potato?"

"Today is a great day for mashing potatoes." She replied laughing.

Naomi got out of the car, retrieved her things from the back seat, and then turned to bid Molly farewell.

"You will write, won't you?" Molly asked. "If you don't, I will always wonder how your Amish journey ends."

"Oh yes, I will write. I must know what seasoning you put in your mashed potatoes today. I want to know how your story ends also and if there will be a sweet potato man after you throw out the mashed potato one."

Molly laughed and then lit another cigarette. "Be safe, Naomi. I will eagerly await a letter from you."

"Good bye, Molly. God keep you in his care and I will write as soon as I have a permanent address."

Osceola Black Lightning, who had been off delivering the hounds of Heaven back to God's kennel, returned to Earth and stood on the highway shoulder with Naomi as she waited for a ride. The syrupy voiced angel had changed clothes while she was in Heaven. She had to. God's hounds had used her leg and gold stilettos for a substitute fire hydrant. Her designer camouflage hunter's clothing was in God's washer and Mrs. God was cleaning her shoes. In Osceola's mind that was the least she could do; it was her dogs.

Now, Osceola was dressed for colder weather and hitch hiking. She wore sensible denims and a pair of designer, navy blue, opened toe stilettos. She also wore a denim jacket with just a few diamond studs on it. She didn't want to look over kill in her down home look. For a hat, she had chosen a navy blue felt panama type one that only had a couple peacock feathers gracing it. She had toned her appearance down for the day. Even her huge handbag only had a few emeralds on it. She had decided that she did not need to flaunt herself in front of those less fortunate who had to wear three yards of cheap, discount store, gray fabric. She was trying to be considerate, even though the white caps couldn't see her. However, she was still trying to figure out how the cigarette puffing, Molly woman had been able to see her. Maybe she was an angel also, just in disguise. That was the only explanation that she could come up with.

Osceola pulled out her long nail file from her bag and worked on her nails while she waited with Naomi for another ride. As she stood there filing her nails, she thought of her long legged Jack Rabbit that she was going to get to spend two days with when this boring mission was over. She could just feel his long legs and arms around her. God wasn't going to be happy with the little, itsy, bitsy bit of fornication she had planned. As a good old, choir singing, Bible thumping, Baptist girl, she would pray and repent just as soon as they were done. She had given it a lot of thought. God couldn't hold it against her if she repented quickly. However, she knew she was not going to be sorry for her sin of fornication. How can you be sorry for pleasure and bliss? That was what it was going to be like in Jack's arms. She wished this gray cap would get down to business and get her act together so she could move on with her own life.

CHAPTER FIVE

Rachael's Harvest

O nce on the main highway, Naomi received a series of short rides going this way and that way. She really didn't have any destination in mind. Wherever they said they were headed, she accepted it as the way she was to go. It was a long day with a lot of idle chatter with strangers. After Molly, she just told everyone she was headed for a friend's place in another settlement. That seemed to satisfy all inquiries except for her last ride for the day in a gold sports car. A huge black woman with a syrupy, sticky, fly catching voice was driving. She asked her everything from why she wore her white ribbons and cap to how they took baths when they had no plumbing in their houses and did she make love only on Saturday nights. She had been extremely glad to get out of her vehicle. She almost had a sore throat from answering so many absolutely ridiculous, rude questions. The huge black woman, with perfectly painted nails and hair, had almost driven her crazy. Also, the denim suited, huge woman in a peacock feather hat had kept a very long sharp nail file lying between them. Naomi had been a little fearful. She quickly thanked God for keeping her safe upon getting out of the gold, two seat sport car with shiny things, like bits of glass studded on the steering wheel. The woman drove ninety-eight miles an hour and didn't stop for red lights or stop signs. Naomi was sure that she had ridden with an English crazy woman.

After her last ride, Naomi found herself a few miles from the Tennessee line. Exhausted, she sat down on a highway embankment just past the shoulder of the road and watched the sun go down. Twilight and peace overtook her. After five years of night mares, she was exhausted enough that she was sure she was going to be able to sleep. She was too physically tired to think, feel, or have night terrors. She was pleased with the possibility of peaceful rest. Every night till now, she had relived in her sleep Joel pushing her down, her baby Mary gasping and dying, and the horror of being told in the hospital by strangers that her five year old son was dead.

Naomi had spent five years pacing the floor at night praying to be forgiven for sending Adam out into the rain to get his grandparents which resulted in his taking pneumonia. She questioned herself as to whether she had caused Joel's madness as his mother, Martha, insisted to everyone in ear shot. She questioned whether she had failed her husband in the bedroom. Was that the reason he had once more wandered off and was possibly frequenting harlot women? She had not forgotten the disease she had to take a long regimen of antibiotics for. Over and over, she recalled grabbing Joel's arm to try to prevent him from wandering off. The grab caused her to be pushed down. Did she cause the death of her infant, Mary? Everyone insinuated she was to blame. Nightmare memories haunted her.

As the sun tipped below the horizon, Naomi felt her eyes trying to desperately close in sleep. Climbing over the farmer's fence beyond the embankment, she made herself a bed on a flat hay bale and fell fast asleep. She did not see Osceola Black Lightning spread an invisible quilt over her and then sit down on the edge of the bail to file her nails till morning and guard her from wolves, snakes, and any male perverts passing in vehicles on the highway.

Stopping her filing for a moment, Osceola looked at her sleeping Amish charge and then using the nail file like it was some sort of wand, waved it over Naomi stating. "Pleasant dreams for the night. God has placed you in my care" Then she looked to the north grinning and added. "If your soul hears me tonight, my long legged Jack Rabbit, I want you to know that I will soon be heading your way. Lay out my fishing rod and change the sheets on your bed."

Lost in the land of dreams, Naomi saw herself baking sourdough bread and spreading it with apple jelly. It was a pleasant dream, free from Joel, Adam, Mary, and the Amish community that had shunned her. She dreamed of a farmer's market and strangers eating her bread. A woman with a Bible, in dress similar to hers, befriended her and told her to create a new world for herself, a world of quilted magic. Her dream was pleasant and she slept the night away in peace.

In the wee hours of morning, Naomi woke to the feel of someone's hand shaking her. She opened her eyes and quickly sat up.

"Good Morning traveler, the sun is up! Might I offer you breakfast and a cup of hot coffee in my kitchen?" A sixty plus looking, tall woman in a long, dusty pink, plain dress with a high neck and long sleeves asked. Around her waist was tied a crisp white apron. Her white hair was pulled back in a bun like her own. However, she did not wear a white, Amish head cap with ribbon streamers like herself.

"Good morning," Naomi stated. "I hope you don't mind, my last hitched ride stopped here and I was so tired, I fell asleep on your hay bale."

"Jesus was born and placed in the hay to sleep. You share an experience with him" The tall respectable looking woman stated smiling.

"Jesus must have slept well in the hay. I know I did on this hay bale. I experienced most welcomed rest and pleasant dreams." Naomi replied standing up.

"I bet Mary, our Christ Child's mother, would have liked to have showered after a night in the stable's hay. Might I offer you the use of my shower? I am Rachael."

"I am Naomi and I would feel quite blessed to have a cup of coffee and a shower. I have traveled far fleeing a nightmare. Sleep on your hay bale has renewed my strength and now you offer me further blessings. I am most thankful."

"Believe it or not, my hay is blessed. All the farmers about this farm had poor crops this year. God caused ours to yield. He created this blessed bale of hay to be overlooked and left behind for you a bed."

"I believe in blessings when we are in alignment with God's path for us. I am asking God to bless my crop next summer. It will be sourdough bread, apple jelly, and handmade aprons to sell in the new land I journey to. My old life passed away and now it is time for me to make my home among strangers. I dreamed about it last night," Naomi replied.

"Come," Rachael stated helping her with her tote bag. "I am Pentecostal Holiness. What is your religious persuasion?"

"I am Amish and a traveling community of one. I am on my way to a new promised land of God's choosing to start a new life and business for myself." Naomi replied walking across the field toward a sprawling white farmhouse with Rachael. "I will pray and accept into my arms whoever he chooses to join me in prayer and in my new Amish life."

"We are spiritual pioneers and do prepare the way of the Lord. I am a Pentecostal Holiness minister." Rachael stated.

"A minister . . . You are a minister and not your husband?" Naomi asked in shock.

"Yes, God called me to preach and my husband, John, supports me in my work. We have a little church in the next town with about fifty members."

The two women did not see Osceola Black Lightning walking behind them, dressed for the morning in purple, mule stilettos and wearing a purple, Hawaiian floral morning dress. In an annoyed, syrupy, sticky voice Osceola muttered talking to her boss.

"I am walking thru a field of plant stubble, cow crap, and dirt. Are you happy God? This definitely is not Paris! Just look at that home sewed, cheap fabric dress that farm wife has on. She is another three yards of fabric hick. I am used to better than this. Good old Baptists know how to shop the mall and dress nice. You are rubbing my nose in the gutter of life, God. I am not a white cap. I am a Paris and New York City girl."

"My Amish elders say a woman's place is in the home, at her husband's feet, and must sit in the rear at services." Naomi threw in the conversation.

"Well, Sweetie, men would love to keep a woman in a position of servitude and under their thumb. However, there are a lot more women that serve God, than men. God uses willing workers. I am a woman, but I am also a willing worker. He has chosen to call me to the ministry to preach His word. I am God's way of shaming the men who are not answering their calls." Rachael replied.

"So, it is alright with your God for women, like you and I, to step ahead of men and assume their roles once they have abandoned them?"

"Come . . . ; let's get some breakfast and a cup of coffee. We will discuss the subject as we eat. My husband has already left for town to sell our harvest and buy supplies for the coming winter. It will just be the two of us. Our son, Mark, lives in Paducah and our daughter in Nashville."

"You just have one son and a daughter?" Naomi asked being used to the Amish families having large numbers of children.

"Yes, just one son and one daughter. Do you have children?"

"My husband and I are now childless. The Amish community that I have just fled insists that I have the curse or wrath of God on me." Naomi replied.

"You have left your husband behind?" Rachael questioned. She did not believe in divorce.

"No, my husband has disappeared. Five years ago he wandered off in a morning rain. He was hearing voices. I have not seen him since. He is presumed dead. You English call his craziness, mental illness. We call it mental madness. My postman believed him to be schizophrenic. I have prayed for five years for answers and for him to return. I can no longer sit and wait for him. I must work to feed myself. I have put him and his craziness in God's hands and am now walking forward towards a new day and a new life. My husband embraced his mental darkness sent by Satan. I cannot embrace his darkness by waiting. I am moving forward in the light of God's love."

"Like you, I am plagued by Satan's darkness in someone I love. It is my daughter that belongs to Satan. She lives a gutter, white trash life in Nashville. She has three children and lives with a man she has never married. She defies all moral standards and I am very much ashamed of her and have the right to be."

"I am sorry! It sounds as though she is in sin's deep, dark pit of fire."

"That she is! I preach Hell hot and a place to flee. She, in defiance of me and what I stand for, goes swimming in the lake of fire like it is a great swimming pool."

"After a child is an adult, you must turn them over to God and go on with your life. I married my husband, Joel, when I was but a child. I was fifteen, a couple of days from being sixteen. I had to grow up this last five years and turn my husband over to God and leave him there. I am in my moving on without him time. I am leaving my five year absent, lake of fire swimming husband in God's hands and I am not taking him out. I have done all I can do!" Naomi stated.

"That is a good point, Naomi. I keep trying to help my daughter and that is taking her out of God's hands. I will wash my hands of her craziness and the man who shares the gutter with her. I will write her tonight and tell her so and move on. Your words have shown me my error. Once you pray, leave your problems in God's hands not taking them out. It has been frustrating helping my daughter over and over and her always using me and what I have to further her gutter life. I have members in my church who need and want my prayers. My daughter does not. I have just now put her in God's hands and will not remove her anymore. You are my witness in doing so. I will move on just as you are."

"You may hold me up in prayer, Rachael. I have no one and would cherish your time spent in intercession for me. For five years, my Amish sisterhood has told me that I am not fit for God to wipe his feet on and that I will never amount to anything. I need a friend and I am telling you the absolute truth in God's sight, it was my husband who was cursing my marriage with his sins."

"I understand, Naomi, members of my own immediate family hold my daughter's sins against me. She has stolen from them, assaulted them, and shamed me beyond belief in their eyes. They insinuate if I had been a better mother, she would not have turned from me and my religion and righteous ways. I have suffered the loss of my brothers and sisters due to my daughter's dark choices."

"When I was told I could not attend church; that was the worst. My Amish community felt they could deny me God." Naomi replied. "God is my friend and he guides and directs my path. That path has led me to you."

"I have had my share of holier than thou individuals telling me I cannot preach because I am a woman and that doing so is an abomination to God. I have worked physically and paid for three acres of land and have built a chapel on it to speak in. I have fifty members now. You must do the same, Naomi. Create yourself a new little Amish world to dwell and serve God in. Do not let anyone tell you that you cannot. Don't let any man or woman stop you."

"I see why God has guided my path to you. I need your friendship, words, and prayers desperately, Rachael."

"I wish I could find someone like you for my son, Mark. He says he can't find a woman with strong will like me and that is the reason he has not married. Unlike his sister, he is a decent man and I am proud of him. However, my husband is a bit of a red neck and is at odds with my son. He feels our son is homosexual because he is twenty-eight and has never married. I don't know whether he is or isn't. Who am I to point a finger at one of God's creatures that has possibly been made a bit different? Mark is just as good as my daughter is evil, although he doesn't come home as often as I would like. Also, my daughter uses him and he just can't seem to see it."

Reaching the farmhouse, they entered and Rachael showed Naomi to her back bathroom in the sprawling farm house, showed her how to work the shower knobs, and laid out towels for her. Naomi showered quickly and then made her way to the kitchen where Rachael pointed to a spot at the table where a steaming cup of coffee and a plate of eggs, toast, and bacon awaited her. The same was placed at the opposite spot.

"Would you like to say Grace?" Rachael asked.

"I would be honored to do so," Naomi stated bowing her head, closing her eyes, and folding her hands.

"Father of the morning, I welcome you to share my day. Thank you for this food shared with me from Rachael's harvest and hands. Bless her kitchen with the breaking of many loaves and fishes to others. May her cupboards be overflowing with abundance just as the baskets were when Christ performed his miracle! I am but one of her multitude partaking of her miracle. I thank you for her. This morning, I ask that you take her daughter into your hands and hold her there till she is remolded or discarded by you. We will not pray for her again, or remove her from your hands. She is yours. For Rachael's son, Mark, I ask that the right mate for him enters his world and that he returns home to Rachael. Give Rachael's husband a fair and abundant price for his crops today. Increase Rachael's church members to one hundred this fall as a sign she stands holy and acceptable in your sight. Last of all, Father, nourish our bodies and let us walk forth into the morning, blessed by the sunlight rays of your love. Amen."

~   ~   ~

Osceola

Osceola Black Lightning stood in the kitchen watching as the two women prayed and then ate together. Standing there, she had sudden inspiration. Leaving the two three yards of fabric women, she flashed thru the morning to a construction site where she positioned herself in front of a port-a-john with her nail file held to swish and sway.

"Naomi asked that her friend's congregation be doubled. I think I can handle that. God is short of angels and I am already here. Why not strut my stuff." she muttered in her syrupy voice. She glanced about at all of the rough, sleepy eyed men arriving for work. Two thirds of them had been out partying the night before.

"Fifty new church members coming up for the Pentecostal Holiness woman's chapel to show her Naomi is what she says she is." Osceola stated finally finding something she could do for her white cap that up to this point had been boring the Hell out of her.

Raising her nail file to eye level, she waved it in the morning sky making some interesting little swishes and sways over the construction worker's only port-a-john. She grinned knowing each of the fifty or so workers would use it sooner or later in the day. She smiled at her ingenuity. The toilet's door had just become the entrance to hell. Anyone who opened the door and stepped inside would instantly have his eyes opened and he would see himself standing in the lake of fire, feel the pains of burns, and see his children, family, or friends burning, scorching, and frying with him screaming in pain.

Some good old Baptists handed out Bible tracks. She handed out experiences. A taste of Hell was more convincing that just reading about it. She was pleased with herself. Then, swishing her nail file, she dressed herself in a traditional white angel's robe and halo to go with wings of gold. She knew the rough neck construction workers, who never read their Bibles, would expect to see an angel that way. She then grinned and waited. She would rescue each from Hell and set all of them to walking on the straight and narrow, after they had been sufficiently scorched a little and were begging and promising anything to get out of the fire. She, as their saving angel, would tell them to be at the altar of Rachael's church on Sunday or they would be back in hell by Monday. That was her plan. She didn't have time to send one measly soul at a time to Rachael's church altar. She was a death angel who transported large numbers. Fifty new members at once for Rachael's church was no big deal.

~ ~ ~

Rachel

Rachael opened her eyes, "Thank you, Naomi for your prayer. It touched me! Now, let us eat."

So, the two continued their earlier conversation.

"Tell me about your daughter, Rachael, so I may get to know you better as my friend."

"I have spent years on my knees concerning her. She ran away when she was fifteen with a male hitch hiker who wandered onto our farm here. He is a tattoo freak and claims to be an artist. She has had three children by him. He refuses to marry her. If it wasn't for food stamps and her working at a nursing home, part time, they would starve to death. They have been thrown out of apartment after apartment for not paying their rent or utilities. She doesn't want her children, but hangs on to them for the food stamps she gets for them. He wanders in and out of my daughter's life at his convenience. Once he walked away for two years. She didn't hear a word from him. Then he suddenly reappeared with a wad of cash which he blew on tattoo equipment. He didn't give Angela a dime or spent any of it on their kids. She is a blind fool who lives and breathes him. Half of his face is tattooed plus most of his body. He is very frightening looking. I think he has a past that he is running from and was possibly in jail those two years. I told Angela to never bring him here to the farm. I am afraid of him and so is my husband. He drinks and lives a wild, gutter existence in Nashville's bar scene. He has been arrested a couple times for indecent exposure and disorderly conduct. My daughter is just like him. She is immoral, lazy, and a user of anyone or any program that will give her a free ride."

"She is now in God's hands. We will leave her there. Do you pray for the tattoo man?"

"I used to, till I had a dream. I saw him in my sleep with Satan's head on his shoulders. I cannot see wasting prayers on the Devil or his demons. My daughter's choice of a man is that evil."

"I agree with you. Our prayers are not to be offered for fallen angels." Naomi stated and then placed her napkin on the breakfast table being finished. "I must be traveling on now and I will pray for you and those coming to you that need you. You pray for me and the business I will start. Neither of us need waste our prayers on Satan. Let God judge and deal with fallen angels!"

"Well put, Naomi. My time spent praying for Angela can be spent in better pursuits for God. I assure you I have left her in God's hands this morning. You, I will pray for. I know you are walking in the pursuit of righteousness."

"Sometimes we are too close to our problems and it takes a stranger to see clearly for us. I need you and your prayers to see closely for me. In return, if you are willing, I will pray and see closely for you." Naomi replied.

"First on my list Naomi, is my son Mark. I want him to find someone special, decent like you to love. Secondly, he is always picking up the pieces for Angela when something goes wrong. She uses him big time. I would like him to let his sister and her problems go, just as I am this morning. She needs to grow up and stand on her own two feet. Mark doesn't stand a chance as long as his sister keeps dumping her kids on him for weeks and sometimes months. No woman he meets is going to put up with that once they get to know Angela. To be blunt, Naomi, he needs to see his sister for what she is and realize that if he wants a wife, a home, and children, he is going to have to discard his gutter trash, leach of a sister. Her children would be better off if they were adopted out. I pray for them to go into the welfare system and be adopted out for their benefit. Being raised by strangers is their only hope for a half way decent life. Mark takes his money, gets lawyers, and sees that they go home to the stench I have prayed them out of."

"I will pray for your Mark to let go of his sister and see her manipulations through clear eyes."

"I will pray for you, Naomi, to hear one way or another concerning your husband that he is either dead or is in some distant city and has abandoned you. If he has an abandoned you and taken up with another woman, you have a right to a divorce in God's eyes. I do not say that to many individuals."

"When the answer comes, Rachael, I will either divorce him or declare him dead in the courts and go on with my life. There has been no word from him for five years."

Rachael and Naomi enjoyed their couple of hours together. Then Naomi returned to the highway. Refreshed of soul, Naomi decided to journey to Paducah where there was a quilt museum and a farmer's market. Rachael had told her about the two and the river that ran beyond them. Naomi loved quilts, so it seemed a good place to journey to and start over. Plus, she could sell her bread and jellies at the farmers' market to help support herself.

Before leaving, Rachael offered Naomi her son's phone number in Paducah for a contact. Naomi turned it down, explaining that she was still married. She told Rachael that she did not feel it proper for her to call on a man or have a male friend for that reason. She would befriend women till her problems were resolved.

On parting, Rachael handed Naomi a small church brochure with her address and phone number on the back. The two women hugged and parted as friends. Naomi tucked her new friend's address away in her pocket along with Molly's.

A car with a cross on the window stopped on the highway beyond the hay bale giving Naomi a ride into her future. Another huge black woman, who looked a lot like the one the previous day, stopped for her. She, however, was driving a 1965 baby blue Ford Mustang. Between its bucket seats lay a huge black Bible. The woman told her that she was Baptist and that her father, when she was growing up, had been a Baptist minister. Naomi was quite taken with the syrupy, sticky sweet southern voice she had. The woman turned on the radio and sang soprano accompanying a gospel music group. She really got into the moment when the group started singing a modern gospel song that went: You better call on God on Sunday or meet the Devil on Monday. Naomi found her to be quite amusing. Living in the Amish settlement, Naomi had met very few black skinned people. She wondered if they all had that sticky, syrupy, southern voice. There was one bad thing about riding with her. She smelled strange, like the stench of over roasted, burnt, scorched meat.

CHAPTER SIX

The Wedding Chapel Minister

After leaving Rachael's farm in Missouri, Naomi's next ride with the black skinned, Baptist woman took her across into Tennessee a couple towns down. There she was let out in front of a small Baptist church with a cemetery beside it. She stood there on the highway shoulder waiting for another ride. She did not see an older, white headed gentleman from the Church by the cemetery walk up behind her.

"Good Morning," A man's voice greeted behind her.

Naomi turned toward the voice and returned his greeting, "Pleasant morning to you."

"Where are you headed? I was about to get in my car and leave the cemetery just now. I spotted you out here. It isn't safe for a woman alone to be hitchhiking." He stated.

"I am traveling with God. I am safe!"

"I have been on a few adventures with him myself. I am Reverend Beecham and I was once a missionary in Haiti."

"Your adventure with God sound exciting. I have heard of Haiti. My journey is a pilgrimage towards peace and a new life in Paducah. I am Naomi Toombs."

"Peace will come to those who seek it. I share that journey with you. I am seeking peace and for my heart to live again. I have not had a peaceful night's sleep since my wife died." He replied.

"Satan wishes to rob God's people of their peace and sleep. The Devil picks on those who have been traumatized. I know."

"Where are you headed?" He asked.

"Paducah, Kentucky. I am a quilter, bread baker, and jelly maker. I plan to go into business and create myself a new world there to live in, hopefully a peaceful one in which I can sleep." She replied.

"I gather someone has told you about the quilt museum and the farmer's market there." He replied.

"Yes, I hope to find peace and a new life in the town by the river." She replied. "God seems to be pointing me there as well as those I meet. My last ride was with a huge, black woman with a marvelous high voice who sang to me about a great river that flows by the throne of God. I took her song as a sign that I am to camp on the shores of God's river which is in Paducah while he solves my problems and works out the details of my future."

"A sign and a calling, I understand that. I was called to Haiti and everyone I met had a contact for me there or spoke of the place. I was your age at the time and working in a Bible college bookstore in Springfield, Missouri. My wife walked into the bookstore one morning with two tickets to Haiti. She had won them playing some radio quiz game. She didn't know that I was hearing a call to go there. I was afraid to tell her. She was a city girl and used to dress shops, manicures, and her parents spoiling her. We took the trip and never came back. I opened an independent Baptist Mission and we prospered in the land of poverty winning many souls to Christ."

"I will prosper in Paducah. I am a hard worker and will create a world from nothing. I have one change of clothing in my bag, a starter for sourdough bread, and my thimble, scissors, and needles. God will take my sourdough starter and multiply it like Jesus did the loaves and fishes." She added.

"You and I have a lot in common, Naomi. I am heading for Nashville. May I give you a safe lift that far?"

"God and I thank you. Yes, I will ride with you."

After walking with the elderly minister to the cemetery parking and getting in his blue compact car, they continued their conversation as the minister exited the cemetery parking and drove.

"May I ask why you are traveling so light?" The elderly, white haired man with a Bible on the seat next to him asked.

"I travel light because I must walk or catch rides. God will provide for me once I reach his destination."

"I started over myself a few years back. My wife became ill and we returned here to the states for medical care for her. She died after six months of being treated for cancer. I just can't go back to Haiti without her. I now spend my afternoons and evenings as a wedding chapel minister on the outskirts of Nashville. I return to the cemetery here in the mornings to sit with my wife. I just can't seem to let her go. I slept next to her for forty-five years. How do you move on and sleep alone?" He replied speeding along toward Nashville.

"I am sorry about your wife. However, it is a great blessing to go be with the Lord. You have had what men dream of, a long marriage that was happy and with the right woman. I was not so blessed or smiled on." Naomi replied.

"I am a minister. Would you like to tell me your troubles so I can pray for you later after we have parted?"

"My husband walked away from our farm field five years ago, climbed a fence, and disappeared on the black top that ran behind our place. He had a mental madness. He would disappear and then return not knowing where he had been. This went on for over five years. The last time he left, five years ago, he did not return. Before leaving, he pushed me down killing our unborn daughter. I was seven months pregnant with her. She lived fifteen minutes in my arms. My frail asthmatic son ran for help in the rain, caught pneumonia, and died a week later. I lost my husband, my daughter, and my son in one week. I have been thru five years of hell and grief waiting for my mad husband to return. I decided yesterday, that I had waited long enough. I walked away and here I am in your car traveling into my new life."

"I am so sorry. It sounds like your husband might be schizophrenic. I respect you in your move forward. It is hard to walk away from the familiar."

"Thank you!" Naomi stated. "I have been alone with no one to turn to for five years. My Amish community shunned me, at my mother-in-law's insistence, saying I was not a good wife and that I caused my husband Joel's madness. She also insisted that the death of my children was the wrath of God falling on me. Joel brought the curst to our house, not me. I have been faithful to God and my prayers."

"I would say that your mother-in-law did not want to face her hand in your husband's madness. Mothers want their children to be perfect. It does not always work out that way. God has given men free-will choice. Some choose darkness. Your husband may have chosen darkness."

"Do you have children?" Naomi asked.

"My wife and I were not blessed with children. However, all the children in Haiti became ours. We loved, helped, and prayed for all the ones that made their way to us."

"It takes a big heart to love children not your own. Every time I see a child, I run from them. They remind me of my loss. Until the last week or so, I have not considered more children. Like your wife, I cannot let them go. Even when I resettle, I plan to have their bodies moved to a cemetery close. I wish to visit their graves as you do Mrs. Beecham's."

"I am sorry for your loss, Naomi. We are alike, aren't we? Both of us need to move on, but we just can't quite let go yet."

"I will pray that God moves you forward and that He gives you a new vision for the future, a new purpose more in line with your calling. You pray the same for me."

"Someday, Naomi, our paths will cross again. When they do, we will share how God has given us new vision. Here is my business card. On the back is a number for my nephew, Dan Maynard, who is an attorney in Paducah where you are headed. He could help you to get your husband declared dead or a divorce if he is alive. When you feel the time is right, call him and tell him that I sent you."

"Goodbye, Rev. Beecham. Thank you for the ride and the sharing of our lives. One day, I will come to you, when I prosper, and make you apple dumplings. You are my new friend and father. Like your Haitian children, I am an orphan who needs your love."

"Perhaps one day, we will fly to Haiti together. I would enjoy introducing you to all my friends there as my adopted daughter."

"I would like that. I will pray for you daily. You pray for me!" She stated as she got out of his car in front of the bus station in Nashville. Rev. Beecham also got out and accompanied her inside where he purchased for her a bus ticket to Paducah.

Sitting down on a bench to wait for the bus to Paducah, Naomi thought about her three new friends, Molly, Rachael, and Reverend Beecham. Her move forward had brought her new friends who had blessed her, not cursed her. She felt her new life had God's approval. She was thankful.

~   ~   ~

Osceola

When Reverend Beecham stopped in front of the bus station, a third invisible, person got out of his car. Osceola Black Lightning entered the bus station and walked around while Naomi and the Reverend said their goodbyes. She was bored to tears and looking for something to amuse herself.

She spotted a very petite little white haired lady about the Reverend's age sitting and reading a small new testament waiting on her bus to arrive. Naomi recognized her as having been a heart attack victim she had transported over about six months prior. God had sent her back to Earth telling her that her work as a soup kitchen missionary was not complete yet. Having no family, she had just been released from a long term rehab facility and was catching a bus home to the city she had grown up in and went to Bible College in. Unable to do soup kitchen work now, she was hoping to possibly get into one of the city's religion oriented nursing homes to live out what was left of her life. She was eighty. Osceola Black Lightning smiled as she pulled her long nail file from her hand bag. Sometimes God wasn't too swift in the match making business. She knew because she couldn't get thru to Him that her Long Legged Jack Rabbit was the one for her. The Reverend was single and she was single. Both were Christians and had gone to Bible College. They were about the same age. Why not?

She glanced about to see where the Reverend was and saw him purchasing a cup of coffee from a vending machine to take with him. He had said his good byes and Naomi was seated, bus ticket in hand, waiting for her dog to ride to Paducah. She watched as the Reverend started walking towards the exit where he would have to pass within a foot or so of the elderly woman who was lost in her Bible reading. She raised her nail file to eye level and just as he stepped in from of the little woman, she gave a little swish. The Reverend tripped on his own feet and landed across her lap like a little boy that was about to be spanked.

"Old folks need all the help they can get!" She muttered as the Reverend's cup of coffee hit the floor splashing everywhere.

Surprised, thinking the man was a mugger like many that had come thru the soup kitchen, the little old lady started beating him with her Bible. The reverend scrambled to his feet and started yelling, "I am sorry, I am sorry, I just tripped. See my coffee is all over the floor. I am with that Amish woman over there . . . she's my adopted daughter; ask her. I am a minister."

The little white haired lady quickly stood and pointed her finger at him with her Bible. "Swear on my Bible!"

The Reverend replied, "I swear you have the prettiest blue eyes I have seen in years. There is something about them that I recognize. Where are you from?"

"That is none of your business, but I am from Springfield, Missouri. I went to Bible College there. I have been a soup kitchen missionary ever since. Who are you?"

"I can't believe it. I know you. We worked in the same book store when we were young. My name is Beecham. I was married back then and my wife and I went to Haiti as missionaries."

The little white haired lady put her arms down. "You are just as klutzy as you were back then. Go ask the station attendant for a mop and help me clean your mess up. You may have been the bookstore's assistant manager back then, but you are a janitor now. Get busy. I have a bus to catch."

"I am headed for Springfield. Why not ride with me and tell me all about your soup kitchen years. I have a few stories of my own about my work in Haiti." The Reverend Beecham asked. "My car is parked outside. I have a quick little wedding to officiate at across town and then I am free to head to Missouri. We might as well travel together."

"Not in your dreams, Beecham. I am a righteous woman who doesn't ride un-chaperoned in a man's car. Yes, I remember you, but you could be lying thru your teeth to me. I will ride the bus thank you. Should you ever fall across my knees again, you are going to get one hell of a spanking. I am no one to mess with."

Reverend Beecham grinned at her. "Where did you say you would be staying in Springfield? Perhaps I could drive to Springfield alone next week and possibly meet you for lunch. I will treat you for lunch at the finest soup kitchen in that city to make up for my fall across your knees."

She grinned. "Sorry, Beecham . . . I vowed to God when I was young that I would live a single life and devote my all to him. Eating meals with a klutzy jerk like you is not part of that vow."

Rev. Beecham grinned and held out his hand to shake hers. "I understand."

Osceola Black Lightning shook her head and rolled her eyes. "A perfect match and they don't see it. What a waste of my talents." She muttered in her syrupy, sticky, sweet southern voice as the Reverend Beecham exited the bus station.

Then she heard a booming voice and knew who it was.

"Osceola Black Lightning . . . quit playing around and messing with my plans for men!"

"Uh . . . oh . . ." Osceola replied reverently in her syrupy, sticky, sweet fly catching voice. "Sorry! Keep in mind that I am a death angel filling in."

"You keep in mind that you are not a cupid angel on assignment. Leave the match making to me!"

CHAPTER SEVEN

DAUGHTER OF SATAN

An amply endowed, strange looking woman in her late twenties sat down next to Naomi inside the bus terminal. Her head was shaved and she had what looked like hog rings in her ears, nose, and lips. The female creature weighed at least three hundred pounds and had tattoos everywhere on her body. Her ample endowments looked like they were about to fall out of her low cut blouse. Huge cottage cheese thighs were exposed due to the short shorts she was wearing which looked to be three sizes too small. It was fall and her clothing, in Naomi's eyes, was entirely in-appropriate. She appeared to be purposely trying to make a statement. She had gone to great effort to let as much of her body hang out of her clothing as possible.

Feeling uneasy, Naomi picked up her tote from the floor and secured its handles on her arm and sat it next to her on the bench. For some reason, she felt the trashy looking, heathen woman was a possible threat.

"No need to hang on to that tote so tight. If I wanted to rip someone off, it wouldn't be you. The price of your bus ticket and that worn out grocery tote is probably all you own. Lighten up. I won't bite you today."

"You bite?" Naomi blurted out not thinking.

"Only when it pays me cash . . ." The badly dressed, loud mouthed woman retorted.

"I am sorry. I do not understand!" Naomi replied still holding on to her tote.

"You are definitely from hick city. Men pay cash for sexual favors! It is easy money and that is what I am here for, not the possible ten or fifteen dollars you have on you."

"You are a . . ." Naomi replied in shock. At the same time she wondered why any man would even consider sleeping with a huge beast of a harlot like her. There was nothing attractive about her. She didn't even look like a woman with her shaved head.

"I am a prostitute; if that is the word you are searching for, and a damn good one. What are you, some country hick's legal whore?"

"I am a child of the Most High God and am no man's whore. I am a free woman with no need for a man."

"I bet your damn nights are lonely!" The harlot replied. "My common law husband is on a bus headed here. He has been gone a couple of weeks attending a tattoo expo. I came a little early to the station thinking I might pick up a few extra bucks while I wait. See that construction dude in brown boots over there. He is probably good for a fifty and that nerdy man in Khakis, seventy five. Men, who wear kakis and collared shirts, usually have better paying jobs. The T-shirt and jeans men are losers who have probably called home for bus ticket money."

"Does your husband know that you work a as a harlot when he is gone?" Naomi asked in shock.

"I work a couple legitimate nights each week in a nursing home to satisfy my mother and one fat judge that I plan to get even with in a dark alley some night. He ruled I had to work a steady job after my last arrest for hooking, part of my probation. Otherwise, it was five years in prison for me."

"Caring for the elderly is a good thing!" Naomi replied searching for something to say.

"I don't want to care for my own stinking, white headed mother, much less some strange old farts. My mother, her God, and all those old nursing home farts could all drown in the nursing home Jacuzzi. I wouldn't care. I have three months of probation left. When it is over, I will kiss that old folks home good bye and maybe kick a few canes from some of the white head's hands on the way out."

Naomi gasped thinking of white haired Reverend Beecham and his deceased wife. "You have no compassion for the elderly?"

"They have all had their day. Give them an overdose of sleepers and let them go. My parents are getting there. I would have no regret sending them on to meet their maker. My Victorian mother has been a thorn in my side, all of my life. My father is a doormat and never once took my side when it came to a show down with her on anything. He is a wimpy, hen pecked, pew sitter. I hate him, her, and my brother who is favored by them. He was a perfect 4.0 student in high school and they doted on him. He went off to college and became someone in their eyes. I hated school and dropped out as soon as I was old enough. My parents have always seen me as a total failure. I have made it my mission to see how bad I can make myself look in their eyes."

"Respect your parents and long will be your days." Naomi let roll off her tongue in reply.

"I respect them enough to kick them in the ass if I ever get a chance."

"You are most sinful with your words." Naomi replied.

"Sin is my bag and I am enjoying whoever I can stick it to."

"Bus Seven for Paducah and points north is now boarding at door three. All aboard for Paducah . . . !" A voice on an overhead speaker announced.

"That is my bus!" Naomi stated glad to be leaving the company of the harlot woman. "I will pray for you!" She stated getting up to leave.

"Don't bother, Ms. Farm Hick Bible Thumper. My mother has been doing that for years. It would take a disaster or a miracle in my life for me to change. I do not believe in God and see my parents and others like them and you, as idiots. I love only one person in this life and that is my man, Joe. I would do anything for him including walking the streets for money to buy him whatever he wants. I would kill you, if he asked me."

"Oh . . ." Naomi gasped in shock once more. "You are a daughter of Satan!"

"I absolutely am! Watch for me in your dark alleys. I just might change my mind and take your worn out tote and fifteen dollars, just for the fun of it."

Naomi then wasted no time boarding her bus for Paducah. She did not exchange names and addresses with the Satan woman as she had done the others she had met. Once on the bus, Naomi repeated to herself over and over till the bus pulled out. "Flee from the Devil and he will flee from you!"

Seeing that the harlot, who was now standing and approaching a man offering her services, had mouthed Naomi, Osceola, in her invisibility, waved her hail file above the buzz cut head of the woman with a swish and a sway. Instantly, her two sizes too small, tight shorts ripped down the back all the way from the waist to the crotch. Then a transient man walking in front of her tripped and spilt a nasty cup of green and black chew spit down the front of her low necked blouse. Osceola then did a little quick swish of her nail file letting the transient run and escape from the mad woman before she could grab him and physically assault him.

Putting her nail file away in her big handbag, Osceola muttered to herself. "No one threatens those in my care and gets by with it. You are lucky I didn't snatch your soul and transport it to Hell."

Osceola then boarded the bus with Naomi and sat down behind her a couple of rows back. She pulled a huge black Bible from her designer handbag and began to read to pass the time. As she read, she took her huge nail file out of her bag and began to file her nails. She was a designer dressed, well manicured, Bible reading, stiletto wearing, guardian angel. Her hair was perfectly salon done and she wore a hat that she was sure the Queen of England would pay her a ransom for.

Who says an angel has to run around in a long white robe with bird feather wings on their back and a halo stuck on their head?

CHAPTER EIGHT

Sloppy Dog Kisses

The bus ride to Paducah was pleasant. Naomi had never been on a bus, so it seemed quite wonderful to look out the huge windows at the landscape flashing by her. She felt like she was flying across the landscape like an angel. The experience of riding the bus was a treat like a roller coaster ride was to thrill seeking, English children.

The bus stopped at a little town and a young man in his twenties and in a camouflage military uniform got on. He walked down the bus aisle to where she was seated.

"Excuse me. I was wondering if you would mind if I sit in this seat next to you."

Osceola, a couple rows back, grinned. She was taking care of business and with a little swish and a sway of her nail file, had let the good looking young soldier angel spot the seat next to Naomi.

"Yes, you may sit with me. But wouldn't you rather sit with some of the gentlemen in the back? That would be more appropriate."

"There are no seats available back there. I won't bother you. I just want to close my eyes and sleep between here and where I am going to get off."

"You may be seated." Naomi replied and turned her face back to the window and her adventure, momentarily forgetting the nightmare she was running from.

"Would you mind waking me when we get to Paducah? I am headed there to spend the rest of my weekend leave with my cousin Karen. I haven't slept since yesterday."

"Yes, I will wake you. I know what it is like to need sleep!"

"Are you getting off in Paducah or venturing further north?" He asked politely.

"I am getting off in Paducah where I will contact a Karen Cameron about a possible apartment she has for rent."

"Well, isn't this a small world! Your Karen Cameron is my apartment house owning cousin. You can walk over to her place with me. She doesn't live too far from where the bus will drop us off." He replied taking a good look at her.

"My God is the weaver of my life and you are but another thread on his great loom of mysterious ways." Naomi replied.

Osceola Black Lightning, seated two rows back, rolled her eyes and muttered. "I never get credit for anything."

"Just wake me when we get there. I am Corky Cameron in case you are wondering."

"I am Naomi Toombs."

He then leaned back in the bus seat and closed his eyes.

Arriving in Paducah, Naomi gently nudged the young soldier named Corky, waking him up. After they got off of the bus, they shared some idle chatter as they walked to his cousin's apartment house. The complex consisted of five small apartments in an old three story Victorian white house that had the exterior paint peeling and the lawn needing mowed. Naomi did not say anything, but she was sure, had the owner of the complex been Amish, the exterior as well as the lawn would have been presentable. However, she was in the land of the English now, and they did not seem to have a lot of pride in their lawns and houses.

"You go on up to the manager's unit and knock. I am going to slip around back and visit my dog named Lucky who is chained out back. Karen is keeping him for me till I complete my tour of duty for Uncle Sam." Corky stated pointing to the Manager's apartment.

"You wish to see your dog before your cousin?" Naomi asked thinking he did not have his priorities straight.

"My dog will shower me with kisses and a wagging tail. The most I will get from my cousin if she isn't drunk and can see me, is a hug and a bottle of beer."

Naomi snickered and then replied, "A shower of kisses would indeed be preferable. Enjoy your lucky kisses. I should be so lucky."

Corky grinned and shot back, "I would enjoy it more if those big sloppy kisses were from a pretty girl. I just don't seem to have one at the moment."

"You are quick of tongue. I am sure your heart will race for a suitable girl your age with a sloppy tongue and a tail that wags!" Naomi replied and then blushed, thinking of what she had just inferred.

"Maybe I will return on leave to visit you instead of my cousin!" He retorted to annoy her. Corky Cameron was a male angel who was wondering how she was able to see him.

"I am taken, but your words are kindly noted." Naomi replied smiling at the young man in military uniform. "My husband would not approve of my sharing sloppy kisses with a man who kisses dogs."

"Your point is taken." He stated laughing at her wit. He then left her to go in search for his dog.

Naomi walked up to the door with a sign that read manager and rang the bell. A woman wearing blue jeans and a T-shirt opened the door. She had one wild, red, frizzy, ponytail.

"Yes . . . may I help you?"

"Molly gave me your address. She said that you might have an apartment that I could rent. I am alone and it does not need to be a large space. I am Naomi Toombs."

"Come on in! I talked to my aunt last night. She hoped that you would make your way here. Did she give you the 'BE ALL YOU CAN BE' talk?" The red pony tailed woman asked laughing.

"She did indeed instruct me on the need to create a good life for myself and not to depend on a man. I hope to start that new life here." Naomi replied stepping inside of the manager's apartment.

"Molly said for me to tell you, should you end up here, that she threw her couch potato out last night. She said to tell you that she seasoned the mashed potatoes by peppering him with his clothes on the half un-mowed front lawn, whatever that means."

"She put pepper in her mashed potatoes. Your Aunt Molly rules her world with hot spice." Naomi laughed.

"That she does! No man craps on her."

"Your aunt gave me my first ride on the way here. I will be letter friends with her." Naomi replied.

"Are you married, Naomi?"

"My husband is ill and has been away for five years. We are not currently residing together for that reason."

"I am sorry about that! I would rather have a husband that is ill than one that is a cheat. My marriage broke up about two years ago. I caught him with a whore down in Nashville. I am in the process of getting a divorce when I decide to let it go through." Karen replied retrieving a ring of apartment keys from a hook by the door.

"Adultery is reason for a divorce." Naomi stated while waiting for the red haired woman to slip on a pair of shoes. She had answered the door barefoot. "Divorce is rare in my Amish community and adultery is the only reason for it. We are married till death!"

"I caught my husband with his tramp down in Nashville purely by accident. I threw him and his clothes out on the curb two years ago. I have a right to a divorce, but I am not sure whether I want one. I was in love with my husband and still am, although I won't admit it to any of my family or friends."

"You peppered your lawn with a man's clothes like Molly."

Karen looked at Naomi and snickered. "Molly and I are indeed a like except I don't look like her. I have this awful red hair that no one can explain what gene pool I got it from. You are also right in your assessment of Molly. She sees her men for what they are. I am one of those blind idiots that believe a man's excuses when he tells her he is going fishing for the weekend or bowling with the boys. My husband was a salesman and probably met his tramp on one of his sales trips to Nashville."

"Were the two of you married long?" Naomi asked being polite and joining in on the girl talk conversation.

"What goes around comes around as they say. I met him somewhere around ten years ago. He was newly married and left his wife for me. We met by accident at a service station and just fell in love instantly. I never met his wife, but he always insisted she was a Victorian prude and that he was not in love with her. I can just hear him telling his new woman down in Nashville that I am a prude and he never loved me. He has a line. I called his sales company to get his address in Nashville to send his divorce papers to. They informed me that he had never worked for them. Figure that one out. I went to Nashville to visit a fellow, older teacher who had gone into a nursing home there. Believe it or not, I walked in on my husband and his tramp making love in the second bed in my friend's room. The tramp worked part time at the nursing home."

"I married my sick husband a little over ten years ago. His mental madness started about the same time. He would wander off two or three days at a time and then return. Mental illness is a craziness of his that has brought me much sorrow. No one told me that my intended was mentally crazy before I married him. I was an orphan and the brethren arranged the marriage." Naomi stated.

"My ex now calls begging to come home saying he still loves me." Karen replied as they walked outside the manager's door to climb and take a peek at a third floor apartment. Karen paused for a moment leaning on the railing of the ancient, rambling, Victorian porch to finish their conversation.

"Is he worth taking back? Are his words of sorry genuine?" Naomi asked.

"In my opinion, it is this apartment house he wants to get his hands on. He inherited a small amount of cash five years ago. We used it as a down payment on this place. I have decided that I will burn this place to the ground before I will let him and his Nashville tramp have a dime from it. The down payment was the only money he ever threw in our marital finance pot. I have always worked and never asked him for money. He said he was banking his checks for our retirement some day. I was a blind fool. He and the Nashville whore have three kids, all born during the ten years I was married to him. His checks weren't going into the bank anywhere. He was giving them to his other family."

"Wow . . . I did not realize that English men could be so deceptive." Naomi stated in shock.

"I was madly in love with Joey, to the point of believing anything he said. He told me that I was his soul mate, the only woman he would ever love. I believed him. While he was telling me how crazy he was about me, he was having three kids with another woman. I hate to admit it, but I was a blind fool."

"Do you have a photo of him so I will know him should he come around?" Naomi asked.

"I tore all his photos and our wedding photos up and threw them out with him. It is best not to have reminders sitting around of a nightmare."

"What does he look like?" Naomi asked thinking that Karen's story seemed a lot like her own.

"The night I threw him out, he had a beer belly and a huge cut on his right arm just above his tattoo of a sailor's anchor and a nude woman holding a flag. He always told me he did a stint in the Navy when he was young. However, I never saw any uniforms, photos, or mementos from those days. It was just one more of his lies, I am sure."

"My husband, Joel, was a simple man who had a full beard and walked away in Amish dress. He always returned in his Amish clothing till one day he walked away in the rain and did not return. Tattoos are graven images to us. His body would be free of them."

"Let's get down to business and let the memories of our two yahoo husbands take a hike."

"That is what I have come here to do. I must create a life for myself because my husband is ill and will not apparently be returning home to me. I must learn to support myself in the Land of the English."

"I have a vacant third floor apartment that no one wants because of the three flights of stairs. If you are interested, I could let you have it for half the price of my other units. It is really small. However, it has a good view of the quilt museum, the farmer's market, and the river."

"It sounds wonderful. I do not mind stairs. They are good for the waist-line. I am a baker and sometimes over indulge on bread and cake. I welcome the stairs."

"Well, follow me up these stairs and we will take a look at the unit." Karen replied leading the way. "Do you have children, Naomi?"

"My two children are dead. They sleep in a cemetery back home in Missouri awaiting the resurrection. My daughter was born and lived fifteen minutes in my arms. My son, Adam age five, caught pneumonia five years ago and died the same week my daughter was born and died. It was a terrible week of sorrow for me; plus, my ill husband disappeared into his world of mental madness."

"It sounds like you and I both have been thru ten years or so of Hell. Aunt Molly would say to move forward never looking back. She would tell us to live well and stick our finger in the Devil's eye." Karen laughed climbing the stairs with Naomi following her.

"I seek Heaven's peace and plan to live well. I have done been to Hell and survived. I loved my husband, but marriage to a mad man wandering in and out, was Hell."

Reaching the top, Karen unlocked a door. "Well, here it is!"

Naomi entered and looked about. "It suits my needs well. I will take it."

"Great!" Karen replied taking a peep out of the third floor window and thinking of the many walks she had taken down by the river with her ex-husband Joey. "I loved my husband too. Naomi. Looking back now, I can see the Devil I slept with."

Invisible, Osceola Black Lightning listened to the two women speaking of their husbands' flaws and couldn't help her-self from thinking about her long legged Jack Rabbit and muttered to her-self in her sticky voice, "Hell is being in love with a man you cannot have." Then she began to cry forgetting the two women.

Karen and Naomi stepped quickly to the window. A sudden rainstorm was peppering the apartment's window overlooking the river.

"Where in the hell is that rain coming from? The sun is shining!" Karen stated in shock.

"Some angel must be crying!" Naomi stated looking out and then suddenly recalling her mother using that phrase when she was alive. Naomi had been an orphan since the age of four. Both of her parents had died in a buggy accident. They were hit by a car as they drove the black top to meeting. Somehow, she had survived.

CHAPTER NINE

The Farmer's Market

Naomi settled into her new apartment borrowing a few things from Karen to complete her first round of baking to sell at the Saturday Farmer's Market. She compensated Karen with fresh baked bread for the week. In the evening hours, after Karen's days as an elementary school teacher were completed, the two women chatted and became friends. Naomi was pleased with the first days of her new life and to have a lady friend. She had been so lonely the previous five years, shunned in her farmhouse by her community.

Karen took Friday off from work and took Naomi to garage sales so she could learn how to find the things she needed for her apartment cheap. Naomi was delighted and the women shared a morning of friendship, one of many to come. Naomi had never been to a garage sale before and referred to them as treasure hunts. She was fascinated with all the kitchen items and bags of unwanted quilt scraps. Naomi was sure that God was providing her with the material items she needed to start over as well as create her new business adventure. The money from selling her cow, chickens, and horse was going a long way. She was pleased.

Osceola Black Lightning, on the other hand, was bored to tears with rummage sales. She was a designer girl who shopped Paris and New York, not someone's basement or garage. She was not into purchasing and wearing some-one's else's shoes with their toe jam in them. Although she followed

Naomi around faithfully, she needed something to amuse herself with. Used clothing and baking bread just did not bring her the thrills she needed.

The first day at the farmer's market, Naomi toted her breads and a couple quickly made aprons in plastic bags. It was a test run day to feel out the market and see what people would buy. Choosing a spot next to a man who was displaying gourds, a non-competitor item, she spread a red and white checked tablecloth on the ground. She had purchased the table covering at a garage sale. On the cloth she displayed her breads and aprons. The first couple of hours went well and she made mental note of what other vendors were selling successfully. She felt sorry for the vendor next to her, the gourd man. His items were good for conversation, but not much else. However, she was surprised at how many people were buying his gourd seeds. In her opinion, gourds were useless.

After a couple hours, the gourd man, who appeared to be about her age, spoke to her.

"Would it be an imposition, if I ask you to watch my gourds and seeds till I make a quick trip behind us to the rest room facilities?"

"I will, if you afford me the same privilege when you return!" Naomi replied eyeing the gentle, good looking vendor. She was sure he would fail in his business attempt because he had seemed more intent all morning on talking to all of his customers, rather than making sales. He definitely was not Amish and had a knack for selling and bartering.

"It is a deal!" He stated leaving his blue milk crates of gourds in her care.

When he returned, Naomi smiled and took her turn to make use of the rest room facilities. Walking back to her display afterwards, she was amused to see him sniffing her sourdough bread and then her corn bread. Walking up behind him, she continued to watch for a moment or so. She had forgotten what it was like to have a man saunter thru your kitchen sniffing fresh baked bread and hoping for a hot slice with cow's butter melting on it. She had baked only for herself for five years. She was pleased to watch him and have a good memory call. Her father-in-law, Abraham, loved her hot bread and made a point of calling on the mornings she baked. Joel her husband, however, hated her hot bread. He insisted they keep a loaf of store bought, sandwich bread for him to eat. She never understood that quirk of his. However, the memory of her father-in-law and her bread was a pleasant one.

"Ah em . . .," She muttered to get the gourd vendor's attention and his nose out of her bread. "Does the smell of my breads please you?"

"Please me? God, they smell just like my mother's kitchen. In this moment, I am a little boy about eight hoping for a piece straight from her oven with apple butter on it. Your bread has caused me to have a serious walk down memory lane." He stated sniffing a loaf one more time. "This loaf and that pan of corn bread are mine!" He further stated pulling out a twenty dollar bill and handing it to her.

"I plan to bring raisin bread next week. Should I reserve a special loaf for you?" She asked giving him his change from the twenty.

"You don't make apple fritters, do you? I have not had a decent one since I moved away from home. My mother's baking is one thing I really miss. Your breads and their smell have turned me into a little boy again. You and my mother bake alike."

"I remind you of your mother?" She smirked being totally amused with him.

"My name is Marcus. I am sorry if I have possibly insulted you, comparing you to my mother." He stated taking a good steady look at her for the first time. She was his age and drop dead gorgeous in her simple gray Amish, clothing. He swallowed because she was causing something to stir inside him that he had never felt before. At the same time, she was a version of his Pentecostal Holiness mother. He had made up his mind years ago, that he would never fall in love with a Victorian dresser and religious nut like his mother. He had moved far away from home to escape her straight laced ideas. "Damn . . ." he muttered to himself knowing he was attracted to her.

"My name is Naomi. Do I have something on my face?" She asked reaching up and touching her face. "You are staring at me."

"Forgive me. I was studying your face. I am a people watcher and I didn't mean anything rude by my mother remark. My mother was an expert baker. Apparently, so are you!" He replied. "However, I must admit you are prettier than my mother."

"Your mother could be quite ugly and saying that I am prettier could mean that I am just one step up higher from ugly." She retorted amused at his flustered demeanor.

"A man should never infer that a woman is like his mother. I am off to a bad start with you, aren't I? I apologize." He replied quickly.

"Your apology is accepted. If I should open this loaf of bread and slice it, would you care to join me for a piece? I have a small jar of apple jelly in my tote. Perhaps my bread is better than your mothers?"

"That sounds like a winner to me. However, wait a few minutes. I will run down to the drink vendor and get us a couple cartons of milk to go with it. I always had milk with my bread at home. I want to experience the feeling of being eight years old again, drinking milk and eating my mother's bread."

"I see that you are a child at heart." She replied grinning. "You did not move far away enough from home. It still calls to you."

"I am afraid so. Your bread has caused me to regress. Sometimes, my mother will mail me a tin of sugar cookies. She says if I want bread, I will have to come home."

The rest of Naomi's first day at the farmer's market sped by. Her twelve loaves of bread and four pans of corn bread sold quickly. She was pleased to have only one apron left to tote home. The income from her baking was sufficient to feed herself the next week plus purchase staples to do it again.

Paying close attention to the other vendors, she formed ideas about what to make, how much, and pricing. Next week, she would expand her inventory plus make her new friend, Marcus, an apple fritter. Also, she had been informed she must sell some sort of produce in her stand. She would shine and sell a dozen or so apples for people who were looking for just a quick snack. She was now a business woman with a future and Karen had found her two rich, English women that she would clean house for two days a week.

"I am thru for the day. Thank you for watching my booth earlier." She said when Marcus turned from his customers and looked in her direction. It was about one and the hot fall sun was making itself felt. A few of the other vendors were packing up and leaving also. "Will you be selling seeds next week or just dropping by the market for your bread and fritter?"

"My gourds and I are regulars." He replied grinning and thinking he had a whole new reason for being at the market. He loved the way she wrinkled her shiny nose when she smiled. He also wondered how she got it that shiny. Equally as intriguing was how she remained so cool and collected looking when he was perspiring like a sweat hog. He hoped she did not smell the fact that his deodorant had quit working.

"May I ask why you choose to sell gourds? They are non-edible and pretty useless." Naomi asked picking up her red checked tablecloth from the ground. After shaking it, she folded it neatly and placed in her tote bag. Her earnings for the day were secure in her dress pocket, held close by a large safety pin.

"Uselessness is the whole point!" He replied. "I don't care whether I sell anything. It is the friendship and camaraderie of the people here that I am interested in. The gourds grow themselves in my back yard along the fence giving me a product and a legitimate reason for being here."

"I am sorry, I still do not understand."

"I am a confirmed bachelor and live alone. Coming here on Saturday mornings gives me a sense of family. I was raised on a farm and these vendors have become my city farm friends and family. Most of the booths' proprietors are back yard farmers, farm kid transplants to the city like me. I have a well paying Monday thru Friday job as do most of them. None of us need to sell anything; it is just that getting our hands in dirt is just part of who we are. My useless gourds and seeds secure my social position here. For a few hours each week, I have a home, a farm family, and neighboring farm friends to talk with. Going home to Sunday dinner at my parent's house in the country best describes what the market offers me. Coming here once a week is Sunday dinner."

"I understand now. Back home, you would have been my confirmed bachelor Amish neighbor, Henry Turner. He never married. At forty-five, Henry was still going home to his mother's house for Sunday dinner, even though he had a huge farm. When his mother died, he bought bread from me weekly and found a substitute Sunday dinner to go home to. He would drive his buggy into the edge of the city and eat at a truck stop restaurant. The restaurant was his farmer's market." She replied.

"Your friend, Henry, and I are alike. We seek Sunday dinner where we can find it." He added totally amused with her. He was sure that she probably did not realize that her neighbor, Henry, was probably a closeted, gay man. He was single because he couldn't get free from his sister and her children milking his finances dry continually. He was considering taking a teaching position on the west coast to be free of her. There was a lot of distance between Kentucky and California. He wanted to be free from her and that was the only solution that he had come up with. If he ever wanted a life of his own, his sister had to go. For one thing, she was gutter, welfare trash and any respectable professional woman would dump him after meeting her, thinking he came from the same mold as her.

"The farm children transplants will be my family, also. I will consider my Sunday dinner now to be on Saturday instead of Sunday. Like you, I need a sense of belonging. My new apartment is not large enough for cooking and entertaining. I will look forward to Sunday dinner next week with you and your gourds. However, I will pass on your gourds to eat, but will bring us both an apple fritter to share."

"Welcome to my farmer's market family, Naomi. May I ask why you are living in a flat? I have never heard of an Amish woman living in the city on her own before."

"A flat . . . ?" She questioned with a confused look on her face.

"Apartments in England are called flats. Edgar, the garlic seller down on the end refers to his apartment as a flat. He is a farm kid from another country, England."

"Oh!" She replied simply at the new word. "I have abandoned my Amish community. I do not sleep well at night and I thought perhaps the river and its sounds would help me relax and rest. I am here to make a new life for myself."

"Are you married?" He asked wondering why she had left her community. He had never heard of a woman doing so.

"Yes." She replied. "My husband Joel has not been well. He is away right now."

"I am sorry." He replied disappointed. Also, he was a little peeved at himself. He had just broken off a relationship with a married teacher he worked with named Jenkins. Now he was standing with his heart racing for another married woman. Was he nuts? His affair with Jenkins had not accomplished anything. She wouldn't leave her husband for him. He had asked her to move to California with him.

"My husband has been ill for close to ten years. I had to move because I could no longer run our farm alone."

"I can see why you are starting over. Long term illnesses can drain you in many ways."

"Will you be here in the same spot next week?" She asked politely.

"Yes, till winter comes and the market closes." He replied feeling insanely attracted to her face with its shiny nose.

"Good! I have this idea for making a red spiced apple jelly. I need someone to taste it and tell me whether it is palatable. If I bring you a sample next week, would you give me an honest opinion as to whether it is any good? I am considering making it to sell a long side my bread."

Marcus eyed her as she talked about her spice jelly. She was absolutely gorgeous. At the same time, he knew she had to be a Bible thumper like his mother. How could his heart be racing for a Bible thumper like his mother?

"My mother used to ask me to do the same thing. Corn relish was her thing at church bazaars and county fairs. Every fall she would insist I taste the nasty stuff and give her an honest opinion. I hate corn relish to this day. Some of her concoctions were pretty awful, till she perfected her recipe." He laughed.

"You are perfect. I want an honest opinion. I cannot grow a business on bad products."

"What will I get out of it? It is possible that I may throw up two or three times before you perfect your recipe." He shot back teasing her.

"You will not throw up after tasting my cooking. You will beg for more. Perhaps, I am two steps up from your mother's cooking. Your tongue will be pleased." She replied seriously. "I am an excellent Amish cook and you would not have a problem with my corn relish. You would be like my old rooster pecking at spilled corn. You would peck and peck and want more and more. A fat rooster one day ends up in my pot and I make chicken and dumplings out of him."

"Full of yourself, aren't you!" He retorted loving every word that came out of her mouth.

"I have had no one to talk and share my thoughts with for awhile. Perhaps, I do sound a bit full of myself. I will try not to brag next week."

"Come back just as you are next week with a fritter in your hand for me. Perhaps I like a woman who is full of herself. My mother was full of herself."

Naomi smiled at him. "Your words please me. You know that I am Amish, a baker, and married. Who are you?"

"I am a grower of gourds and a dreamer of dreams. Right now, I see myself moving to the west coast and becoming a hermit. The truth of the matter is, I have a great life and occupation. My life would be even better if I didn't have a leech for a sister. She dropped out of school and continually expects me to step up to the plate when she needs something. You are full of yourself and I see myself as drained, like a half empty glass. My sister keeps tipping me over, like a tea pot, and pouring me out. I just can't seem to get her to see that it isn't too late for her to return to school and be someone. She is on welfare and constantly has her hand in my pocket draining me."

"I will pray that you find a solution."

"Do you like Jazz and Blues?" Marcus blurted out, and then realized she would not, being Amish.

"I do not know. Amish only sing hymns. There are a lot of things in your English world that I am unfamiliar with. Perhaps I like Jazz and Blues. I do not know. Does Jazz hit high notes that break glass? My English postman back home was telling me that some English women sing so high that they can shatter glass. I would not want you singing high notes that would break all my jars of jelly that I plan to bring next week."

Marcus, caught off guard with her reply, broke out into an uncontrollable belly laugh. When he could contain himself, he replied. "It is opera voices that can shatter glass. I might shatter a beer bottle or two by throwing them in a dumpster somewhere, but I guarantee you that your jelly jars are safe with me."

"I will then look forward to listening to and deciding whether I like Jazz and Blues with you."

Marcus suddenly realized that Naomi was a blank slate, in ways. Things he took for granted, she probably knew nothing about. In his mind he could see himself introducing her to the art and culture of his world. She was gorgeous and seemed open to new ideas. He could see himself taking her to the opera and enjoying her first experience of it with her.

"I will bring my portable DVD player next week and introduce you to soft Jazz and Blues while we tend our booths." He replied.

"I will bring you one of the best Apple fritters you have ever tasted and we will eat it mid- morning between customers as we listen to your sounds."

"I will bring the coffee." He replied delighted with his new friendship, but alarmed that his heart was racing for a Victorian prude like his mother, who was married.

"That will be wonderful. I take mine with cream and sugar." She replied smiling at the gourd man who had her heart racing. "May God travel with you thru your week and keep you safe."

"Could I give you a lift home?"

"Thank you for your kind offer. However, I am a married woman and I must walk. I cannot be seen in the presence of a man, other than my husband, unless chaperoned."

"Sorry, I wasn't thinking." He quickly added not wanting to alienate her. He was in love. He knew it.

Naomi took her plastic grocery tote and walked away from Marcus heading home.

"Damn . . ." Marcus muttered to himself. "Her husband is one lucky man. I hope he knows it."

Osceola Black Lightning, who had stood filing her nails all day guarding Naomi, muttered. "You won't be making time with her buddy. I know your history with married women. Mess with me and I will snatch your soul right out of you and make you my assistant on the Eastern Gate where I can keep an eye on you." She then gave a little flick of her nail file and a wind swept thru the farmer's market scattering his packets of seeds everywhere.

"Osceola . . . !" She heard a familiar booming voice yell. "You are there to guard the Amish women, not make the waves of the red sea roll back and then drown the English Egyptians."

"Sometimes, I get a little carried away, God! You know that I am a death angel. I get a thrill out of parting red seas and drowning a few Egyptians now and then. If I am not guarding to suit you, then send someone else. Being a guardian angel is not part of my job description." She yelled in her syrupy, sticky, sweet, fly catching voice. "I am a death angel, remember!"

"Point taken, but cool the miracles." He yelled back.

The force of their unheard voices caused a huge storm to blow up sending the vendors hustling to put their wares away and run for their vehicles. It rained, hailed, and lightning flashed violently. Naomi, however, walked home on dry ground and in the sunshine with Osceola walking behind her.

CHAPTER TEN

Fall Ends Winter Calls

Fall flew by and the Saturday friendship between Naomi and Marcus grew. He became her Saturday morning guinea pig, and she became his once a week steady girl, although she didn't realize it. It was a relationship built on coffee, fritters, and being vendor booth neighbors. The other booth proprietors started referring to them as Marcus and Naomi.

A month after meeting, Marcus secretly purchased her a new folding card table to display her breads, aprons, and jellies on. He told her he picked it up at a garage sale for a couple of bucks. Pleased, she paid him his two dollars. He was happy with his deceit.

Marcus found Naomi to be quite witty, in spite of her lack of an education. However, it was the wrinkling of her nose when she was excited talking to him that got him. The wrinkle was an addictive drug that he could not get enough of. Seeing her only on Saturday was not to his liking, but she did have a husband and he could not get around that fact. He had already become accustomed to the one night a week thing from having an affair with Jenkins, a married professor at the university.

What Marcus could not understand, was why Naomi's husband never once accompanied her to the market, or dropped by. She always arrived at the market pulling one of those old lady, rolling, grocery carts. It was always packed to its maximum and almost more than she could handle. He knew it was a physical struggle for her to pull. In his opinion, her husband had to either be on his death bed, or an uncaring jerk.

The last Saturday at the farmer's market for the fall arrived and ended. Naomi smiled as she watched Marcus clumsily pack up his crates of gourds and then her card table which he stored in his garage and carted back and forth for her every week in the back of his jeep.

"You seem a little distracted today. May I ask why?" Naomi inquired watching him.

"I always hate the last day at the market. I will miss you as well as our other vendor friends." He stated with a solemn face.

"We must flow with the seasons of our lives. Our friendship and that we have with the others will sleep thru the winter, but be reborn in the spring waking to new shared moments like flowers. As I sleep this winter, I will visit with you in my memories and dreams." She replied.

"I am afraid my sleeping thru the winter is not going to be so pleasant or peaceful. Will you miss me?"

"I will not let myself miss anyone ever again. I spent five years missing a member of my family who was absent from me. Missing someone is a nightmare which I do not wish to embrace anymore. I will think of you fondly, but not miss you."

Marcus folded up Naomi's card table for her and placed it in the back of his jeep along with her folding chair he had purchased. He spray painted her gray folding chair red to go along with her red apple theme. She had been quite pleased with it, when he brought it one Saturday morning. He painted his green to go with his gourds.

"I will store our tables and folding chairs till spring." He replied wanting to keep a little piece of her, even if it was just an apple red folding chair and a card table.

"Thank you for being my friend as well as hauling my table and chair back and forth each week. I have needed your help and friendship this fall. You have been a gift from God to me." She stated handing him a couple of gourds he had dropped in the loading.

"How will you spend your Saturdays now?" He inquired hoping for some insight into her winter schedule.

"Until they close for the season, I will visit the quilt museum to get ideas for my aprons next year. I will also start a new quilt for my bed in my apartment. I had to leave my wedding quilt behind when I came here to start over. I miss my wedding quilt which always was displayed on my bed back on the farm. You English use bedspreads and comforters. I have not had time to make my apartment seem like home. I will make a new wedding quilt for my bed. That will be my main Saturday project. My landlord, Karen, has found me work cleaning three English women's houses during the week. On Sunday, I will read my Bible and pray, till I find a meeting house to attend somewhere here. I have heard members of the Pentecostal Holiness church live moral and decent lives. If there is a congregation here, I will attend. There is no meeting house of the Amish brethren here, so I must choose."

Marcus cringed. Religion wise, she was everything he was running from. His mother was Pentecostal Holiness and he had been subjected to all of the straight and narrow he wanted while living at home. He wanted a normal life filled with music, art, and culture which in some forms were looked down on by his mother and her church. Rock and Jazz music had been a sin when he was growing up, as well as swimming trunks, dancing shoes, and movie tickets.

"What will be the pattern for your wedding quilt?" He asked changing the religion subject.

"My old quilt was a wedding ring pattern. My new one will be the same. Someday, hopefully, my husband and I will sleep beneath it and wear it out with love." She replied with a faraway look in her eyes.

Marcus cringed at her reference to a husband beneath a wedding quilt with her. He didn't want to think about her sleeping with someone. That was hard for him to handle. He was in love with her and he had known it from the first day she showed up at the market and spread her table cloth on the ground.

"Naomi, why hasn't your husband ever dropped in here at the market or accompanied you to the market?" He asked finally getting up enough nerve to do so.

"He is very ill, Marcus." She replied simply. "He is away right now."

"How ill is your husband?" Marcus asked. Naomi was always so vague or non-sharing when it came to any information about her husband.

"Very ill . . ." She replied simply not offering any further details which annoyed him a little.

"Is there anything that I can do to help you with him?" Marcus asked thinking she possibly had him hidden away in a hospital bed in her apartment or possibly a nursing home locally.

"Only God can help him, Marcus. He is in God's hands."

"I would be there for you and him, if you would let me!" Marcus replied.

"I know Marcus. You are a good friend. However, there is nothing you can do. Until spring, I will clean houses, quilt, pray, and create a new life for myself here. How will you spend your winter?"

"I am a fairly simple man. I will hang out at the library and the coffee shop on Saturday mornings. I am definitely going to miss your apple fritters." He replied dreading the moment she took her tote and walked away from him.

"You are far from a simple man, Marcus. Your arms remind me of the many hanging limbs of the Weeping Willow tree. Your many arms have been there for me all fall helping me load and unload my breads and jellies. To me you are a tall Weeping Willow delight. Delight fits you. You have been my delight."

"Delight, huh?" He repeated asking.

"Yes, you are my Weeping Willow delight."

"You are so much like my mother." He stated shaking his head. "She used to break a switch from the Weeping Willow in our front yard when I had done something she considered to be a sin. She would switch me and then hug me and call me her little Weeping Willy. Now you see me as a Weeping Willow."

"Weeping Willy. I like that nick name." Naomi stated snickering. "Your mother made a man of you that I find to be a delight. Perhaps next spring I should call you my Weeping Willy."

"Between you and my mother, I don't stand a chance. Maybe I should nick name you my Apple Dumpling."

"You wouldn't?" She asked in shock. "That would be an Amish term of endearment for a wife."

Marcus grinned seeing he had her full attention. "Oh my friend Naomi, you are from this moment forward my Apple Dumpling."

"You cannot call me that. It sounds like an Amish man's words of love for his wife. I am married."

"Well, Weeping Willy is a little degrading for a man of my age. You choose a different nickname for me and I will reconsider mine for you." He smugly retorted. She was wonderful and he just couldn't get enough of her.

"What would you like me to call you?"

"How about calling me Markie-Poo?" He stated to further annoy her.

"You wish me to call you Markie-Poo? That sounds like a mother asking a two year old if they need to go to the outhouse to poo . . . !"

"You are right. Maybe, I wouldn't want to be called crap by you, my Apple Dumpling. You choose a nick name for me." He stated watching her blush.

"You are awful, Marcus. Please do not call me Apple Dumpling again. Someone might hear."

"Weeping Willy is one that I do not wish anyone hearing." He retorted.

Naomi laughed. "Perhaps we should just stick to first names. However, you will always be my Weeping Willy Delight, even if I do not say it out loud."

Marcus smiled and then leaned over and whispered into her ear, "You will always be my Apple Dumpling, even if I don't say it out loud."

Naomi snickered. "Till spring, Marcus, I will think of you fondly and re-member you in my prayers. I must say goodbye." Naomi then extended her hand to shake his.

He took her hand, but did not let it go for a moment. "Goodbye, Naomi. Unlike you, I will miss you this winter. Could I give you my telephone number in case you should need me for some reason this winter?"

"I have no phone, Marcus. I am Amish and live simply."

"Would you consider meeting me at the Library on Saturday mornings? We could have coffee and discuss what is going on in each of our winter worlds?"

"I have found myself a Saturday morning Job thru the winter caring for an elderly, bedfast man from Friday sundown till noon on Saturday. I need the income to feed myself this winter. Thank you for your offer, but I must turn it down. Spring will come, Marcus. Till then, I must bid you goodbye."

"If you ever need money, I will help you." He stated wanting to get his foot in her door which seemed shut to him till spring. "I help my sister quite often."

"A man or woman who does not work to feed them-self is worse than an Infidel. I am not afraid of work and God will see that I have work to feed myself. However, I appreciate your kind offer."

Marcus thought of his trashy sister that wouldn't get off her butt to clean her house, much less work and feed herself. She was on food stamps and in constant trouble with the Division of Family Services for neglect of her children. Naomi was her exact opposite. She needed help, but wouldn't take it. He knew Naomi only had one or possibly two gray dresses because she wore them repeatedly every Saturday. Yet, her worn dress was always clean and pressed. Naomi definitely was not a leech on society, like his sister. Naomi lived simply and paid her own way.

"Well, till next spring, Naomi." He replied reluctantly.

"I will send you my prayers every Saturday morning about the time we usually share coffee and apple fritters here at the market. There will be no need for you to miss me. In my prayers, I will always be with you."

"I guess I will have to settle for that." He retorted. Naomi's words were just like those of his mother. His mother was always telling him that she was praying for him, which meant nothing till now. He now could see that his mother loved him and meant it when she said she would pray for him. However, it was Naomi that he wanted to love him.

"Goodbye, Marcus!" Naomi stated and then turned and walked away pulling her rolling tote.

As Marcus watched her walk away, he was not a happy man. He hadn't known her but for a couple months. However, somewhere during that time of jelly tasting and Saturday morning coffees, he had fallen madly in love with her. Depression setting in, he watched Naomi in her plain gray dress, black socks, clunky black shoes, and funny little white bonnet walk away from him.

When she was about out of sight, he became totally irritated with himself. He knew what misery his sister's choice of a man, who wouldn't marry her, had caused his family. Now he was in love with an unobtainable, married woman who he could not marry. His mother harped constantly to him over the phone how his sister was living in sin. Even if Naomi showed an interest in him, he could never take her home to meet his parents. Fornication and adultery were hot topics with his religious, fanatic mother who was a Bible thumper. Second marriages were not acceptable to her. Should he marry Naomi some day, it would be a second marriage for her.

Although he respected his mother for her clean lifestyle, he had moved away after high school and college to be able to embrace and have what he considered a normal life. Jazz and Rock music was a sin to his mother as well as his occasional bottle of beer. Joining the high school swim team and wearing a male's swimsuit were sins. He had walked a tightrope as a teenager with what he considered to be extremist boundaries. Paducah was freedom to him and he had worked hard to create an educated, normal life for himself in the town. Now, he was in love with an extremist woman of another religious persuasion and she was married. He didn't have a clue what to do about it.

Naomi was about to turn the corner out of view, when it dawned on him that he did not know where she lived. Instantly, he knew he had to follow her at a distance to see where her apartment was. He quickly locked his jeep and then jogged till he had her in his sight again. Staying in the shadows, he followed her. He was shocked to see that she lived in one of the oldest, dilapidated, complexes of apartments in the river town. His sister, in low-income housing, lived in a better place. He was appalled and wondered what kind of a husband would let her live in such a dump. In his heart, he wanted to go pack her up and take her home with him. He had a new home across town in a respectable neighborhood. However, taking her home was not possible. She was married and he was an idiot. Staying a block back, he watched her struggle up the stairs with her rolling tote, unlock a third floor apartment door, and go in. He then returned to his jeep heart sick. Unlocking and getting into the seat of his vehicle, it hit him like a ton of bricks. She was the one his mother had told him was out there somewhere. His mother preached that there was one special someone, for each man and woman, and you should wait till that person showed up. He had not waited, and now she had showed up just like his mother said. At the same time, Naomi was everything he did not want. She was a version of his mother.

The winter was extremely long, or so it seemed to Marcus. Like a stalker, he tried secretly to catch glimpses of Naomi without alarming her or snagging the attention of her ill husband who had to be sitting at the third floor window, possibly in a wheel chair looking out. Naomi had said he was very ill. He felt like a heel eyeing someone else's wife from the shadows of the city. His love for her over road his sensibilities and winter did not silence his wanting of her.

Marcus looked for reasons to bump into her thru the winter months. A couple times he managed to follow her to the supermarket and bump into her. He knew she went to the Laundromat on Saturday afternoons, so he kept a basket of supposedly dirty clothes in his jeep side seat for those occasions. Once he spotted her late in the day enter the quilt museum. He purchased a ticket and entered to steal a few brief moments in her presence. She was always delighted to see him and he lived and breathed for those moments, no matter how brief they were. She, however, always seemed oblivious to his feelings for her.

Oblivious to Marcus and Naomi was a third party in their odd little world. Osceola Black Lightning had cabin fever. It was the end of February and in the middle of a white out blizzard. Osceola's Amish woman, wearing a white cap with ribbons, did nothing but sew, make jelly, and sleep in a locked closet. In total disgust with her going nowhere job, Osceola stepped thru the front door of the tiny third floor apartment not opening it. Outside, on the third floor landing, she took a deep breath and remembered all the exciting nights she had reaped souls, sneaked them across Hell's borders, and transported them to Heaven's shores. She was at the top of her game when God stuck her with her current assignment. Now, she had not been to New York City or Paris in over six months and she was chomping at the bit needing a little mall time to calm her shopping jitters.

"Hey, white suit up there, are you listening?" Osceola yelled angrily with her syrupy, sticky voice. "What am I guarding this white cap from . . . bed bugs or cockroaches? I have had it with the day in and day out watching of jelly pots boil. Do you hear me God? I am sick of standing around filing my nails and twiddling my thumbs. I want you to send me a companion for these long, lonely, winter nights, someone to talk to. This woman goes to bed when the sun goes down. I am bored out of my skull sitting in a dark apartment staring at a locked closet where she sleeps holding a butcher knife. There is nothing that is going to go boo in the night here. Her husband has moved on, way on. The only excitement around here for the last month was when one of her hot, jelly jars slipped from her hands and hit the floor exploding"

A booming male voice replied in an annoyed tone. "Chill out; you sticky, syrupy, loud mouth! I am busy up here."

"I have made up my mind, White Suit! You better send me a night companion or I am jumping ship and heading straight for my long legged Jack Rabbit's fishing cabin up north. You can explain to your man coming thru the Eastern Gate, who is expecting to marry me, why I will have a fornication smile on my face." She yelled back in her sticky, syrupy, sweet, fly swatting voice.

There was a huge clap of thunder which did not normally happen with snow falling. Then there was a flash of black lightning. Suddenly sitting crouched on the snow covered third floor stairs was a wimpy, thirteen year old looking girl in a plaid school uniform. Her brown hair was in a pony tail and she was wearing glasses that had slid down to the end of her nose and were sitting crooked. Trembling from a rough landing, she was holding on to the snow covered railing as though she feared letting go.

"Well, let go of that railing, four eyes, and tell me why you are daring to invade my turf.." Osceola demanded.

"I can't. I am afraid of heights and we are three stories up." The young teen girl stated trembling in her crouched position on the stairs. She was also afraid of being attacked by the huge, frightening, black, woman angel on the landing, who was yelling at God.

Osceola grinned seeing that the very young girl angel was visibly trembling in her presence and holding onto five dog leashes with nothing on the end of them.

"Who in the hell are you?" Osceola asked in her syrupy voice eyeing the eighty pound little wimp.

"I . . . I . . . I am here to walk you." The four eyed girl replied as she straightened her glasses on her nose and then pushed them back up from their slid position. "God told me you are scratching at his door wanting out. I have come down to leash and walk you, so you can do your business."

Osceola began to belly laugh and did so till there were tears rolling down her cheeks. Regaining her composure she managed to ask. "You are here to leash and walk me, like a dog?"

"Yes, Mum! God sent me. I am Heaven's dog walker."

"How do you plan to catch and leash? The most you are capable of doing is throwing a vial of pimple cream at me?"

"If I have to . . ." The girl replied crouching by the railing and staying out of Osceola's reach.

Then Osceola began belly laughing again and thinking. Only God would insult me by sending this pip squeak of a girl to treat me like I am a dog. She looked up to the sky once more and yelled. "Don't expect me to pick you up a designer hat, the next time I am in Paris. Insults will get you know where with me!"

There was no reply.

"What is your name?" Osceola asked in her syrupy, sticky voice trying to sound nicer. She saw that the wimpy girl, wearing a ponytail, was trembling in fear of her.

"My name is Four Eyes Frances." The girl replied sniffling. "My friends call me Frankie. You may call me Frances."

"Well, Frankie Frances, you may call me Miss Osceola Black Lightning." She retorted, teed that the girl would dare to insult her by not considering her as a possible friend. "My friends call me Osceola. You, however, may call me Miss Osceola Black Lightning."

"Your name is too long for me to remember. God told me to call you Big

Mouth."

"He didn't?"

"He did!" The teen, four eyed girl replied.

"I will big mouth Him!" Osceola stated mad. "Quit crouching there and stand up straight. We will fly over to a little spot I know and grab a couple cups of hot chocolate. This town doesn't have a lot to offer on snowy, blizzard nights. About the only thing that will be open is the all night gas station. Do you want to share with me how long you have been sent down here to annoy me?"

"I am to keep an eye on you till your mission is completed, however long that takes. God said to tell you that I am your new companion and if he catches you up north with Jack Rabbit Long Legs, he is going to demote you from Eastern Gate Guard. He said to tell you that your new position as the guard of Hell's Gate will not be a pleasant experience, since you are just about over the hill and are having hot flashes."

"I will hot flash him!" Osceola replied eyeing the imp who had dared to deliver to her, God's number one death angel, a message like that. She turned her face toward Heaven and yelled in disgust. "Why have you sent her? She isn't old enough to discuss my loving Jack or hot flashes with, and I don't have a dog for her to walk!"

A booming voice yelled back, "There is an angel shortage up here. My dog walker is all I have available to send you for a companion. Suck it up!"

"He has sent his dog walker to leash and pet me." Osceola muttered to herself in a huff. "Just wait till I tell Mrs. God on Him. This is angel abuse."

CHAPTER ELEVEN

Spring at the Market

After a winter of torture, spring came and with it the opening of the farmer's market. Marcus was thrilled with the promise of at least one morning a week with Naomi. Married or not, he was in love with her and lived and breathed for their encounters. His pining for Professor Jenkins after their breakup just vanished. He couldn't even remember why he chose to have an affair with her, now. Naomi occupied his every waking free moment of thought.

On the way to the market with his gourd seeds, Marcus sped thru the fast food lane of McDees and ordered two cups of coffee. He had the radio on and his soul was alive and rocking. It had been a long winter sneaking peaks at Naomi. Now, she would once more be his Saturday girl. He felt like a thirteen year old anticipating his first encounter with a girl. Naomi had that effect on him.

Arriving at the market, he claimed their two spots and set up her card table and folding chair and then his milk crates of gourds and display of seeds. Also, he set out some birdhouses he had made from last year's leftover gourds. Then he impatiently waited for her arrival. He felt like a little boy waiting to open his birthday present.

There was still an icy nip in the spring air. His hooded sweatshirt felt comforting. He rubbed his arms to warm himself. Some of the other vendors were still sitting in their vehicles to avoid the chilly morning air. He didn't want to miss seeing Naomi arrive. She was his eye candy and he needed a Naomi fix. She was his drug of choice. He loved everything about her, even her crazy, clunky, old lady shoes.

Suddenly, he spotted her heading down the side walk from the business district toward the market. She had what looked like a gray, heavy cloth shawl wrapped about her and she pulled the familiar rolling tote. Taking off in a sprint, he ran the block between them to help her with her rolling cart and carried items.

"Let me help you with that," He stated reaching her. His heart raced even faster when he looked into her eyes and she smiled making her nose wrinkle and wink at him. He was absolutely positive that she had to be the most beautiful Amish woman that ever existed. Her dark hair was pulled back in a bun meticulously beneath her familiar little white see thru cap with its white ribbons hanging down. She wore her familiar clean and pressed gray dress, black hose, and old lady shoes. His heart felt like butter melting. He had been in the winter of the heart and soul; now Naomi was calling him to life once more.

"Thank you, Marcus. I think I might have overloaded my cart a bit this morning. I was just so excited about today!" She replied releasing her grip on her rolling tote to him.

"I have missed you!" He stated as they started to walk toward the farmer's market with him pulling her load with ease.

"I have not missed you, Marcus. I talked with you and God every Saturday morning as I promised. Missing someone is not a good thing. I spent five years in the land of grieving and missing. I will not return there again. I will love those about me, but I will not let myself walk down the missing path ever again."

"I assume someone came up missing in the past from your Amish settlement?" He inquired on a fishing expedition once more to see why she refused to miss him. "Did your father walk away from your mother, perhaps?"

"Something like that . . . !" She replied not offering any further details.

"I am sorry!" He said thinking that her parents were the reason for her not wanting to miss anyone ever again. He dropped the subject seeing sorrow in her eyes.

"My sorry days have come and gone. Now, I am moving forward with my life."

"Well, my Apple Dumpling girl, I admit I missed you. I have not had a decent apple fritter all winter." He replied.

"I hope you will refrain from calling me that in front of our vendor family. If you do, I will call you Weeping Willy. Our friends might think that you are in love with me and that I call you Weeping Willie because you cannot catch me." She replied sternly. "I am married, Marcus, and your use of Apple Dumpling is disrespectful."

"Ouch . . . you are on my case the first day of the opening of the market. My mother would love you. I have gotten switched many times by her for being disrespectful when I was a boy. I once called her an old, religious, prune face when I was about thirteen."

"Oh . . . that is very disrespectful. What did she do to you?" Naomi asked big eyed. No one in the Amish community got by with calling their mother names.

"When she got thru with my backside, with my father holding me down, my rear was black and blue and looked like a prune face."

"Good for her. You deserved it. Had I been there, I would also have denied you any desert for a month and made sure the other children had huge pieces in front of you. Then, I would have baked prune pie for dessert for the evening meal on the day you were allowed sugar again. You would have eaten your disrespect in front of me."

"You are one step up on my mother. You won't deny me my apple fritters for the next month, will you? My calling you my Apple Dumpling Girl was said favorably, not in a negative manner."

Naomi grinned glancing over at him as they walked. "Perhaps, I should write your mother one day and tell her I have found the cure for your disrespect, the denial of Apple fritters."

"I am not introducing you to my mother! Between the two of you, I wouldn't stand a chance. I can just see the two of you making me a front of the church, pew sitter like my father."

"If your father goes to church with your mother and sits on a front pew, he must be a good man. I assume he must be a minister. The leader of our gathering sits in the front."

"It is my mother that leads my father. He has a very big nose ring."

"At least she has him secured to her and he will not run off and leave her. That is a good thing. I have come to the conclusion that the woman should lead the man and I now approve of nose rings. I might not be having the problems I do now, had I put a ring in my husband's nose the day I married him."

"Well my Apple Dumpling Girl, You just put a ring in my nose any time you feel you are woman enough to do it."

"You are awful, Marcus and should have your mouth washed out for the Apple Dumpling words." She stated pausing and then added. "However, you may call me Apple Dumpling in your outhouse till you get it out of your system. Little boys are permitted to speak their mind if they are in the outhouse back home, with the door closed."

Marcus, caught off guard, broke out into laughter and stood still facing her for a moment. "I am aloud to call you Apple Dumpling all I want, as long as I am in my bathroom at home with the door closed."

"Yes, but you may not use the bad words in your living room, bedroom, or kitchen."

"Naomi, you are wonderful!" He stated snorting. He could just see himself as a little boy being sent to his mother's back bathroom and allowed there to curse and get it out of his system, rather than getting a switching.

"You are wonderful too, Marcus. If you really feel the urge to call me Apple Dumpling this morning, I will watch your vendor spot while you go to the market's rest room facility to do so."

Marcus snorted again. "What about you? Are you going to the market's John to say Weeping Willie?"

"Girls do not use bad words. It is only men and little boys that seem to enjoy foul words."

"You have not met my sister!" Marcus muttered beneath his breath.

"I did not catch your last remark." She added as they started walking once more.

"I have met my master!" He replied trying to cover his remark about his sister.

"That is good! Did you join the church at eighteen like the men of our community do?"

"Er . . . uh . . . perhaps we should change the subject. I want to know what you did last winter. I want you to tell me all about your quilting, baking, the elderly man, and the house cleaning for the English ladies as you call them. I want to know everything, including what you ate for breakfast, lunch, and dinner."

"I wish to know about your winter also." She replied as he pulled her tote into the market display area.

"You did remember my Apple Fritter treat, I hope. I have our coffee ready and waiting." He said as they reached their two spots. After helping her unload her wares, he stepped over to his Jeep, opened the door, and pulled out two steaming cups of coffee from his console and handed her one.

"Thank you. Yes, I brought you a treat."

Marcus grinned at her as he watched her take a sip of her hot, caffeine brew. She was his treat and he was so glad they were back together again. He had decided that, married or not, he would take her in whatever form she was willing to give herself to him.

"I have worked all winter on a recipe my friend from Missouri sent me in the mail. I want you to close your eyes and take a bite, tell me what it is, and if it is any good!"

Marcus closed his eyes willingly, hoping that her fingers would brush his face when she put a spoon of whatever in his mouth. He longed for her touch.

"It better be good, Naomi. I would hate for our market season to start off with me on a puking note." He stated with his eyes closed.

"Open wide . . ." She stated firmly.

Marcus opened his mouth and he felt her slip a fork in his mouth with a bite of a sweet, doughy, apple confection. She then removed the fork and he rolled it around in his mouth, chewed for a moment, and then swallowed. It was Heaven to his taste buds and transported him back to his mother's kitchen on their farm in Missouri.

"Now, open your eyes and tell me what it is and if it is any good." Naomi demanded.

As Marcus was opening his eyes, he saw Naomi reach with one finger and wipe a bit of food from his lips and chin like he was a little boy. It was the most sensual moment he had ever experienced. He wanted a repeat performance but knew it would not be given. Her touch was magic.

"Tell me what it is and if it is good!" Naomi instructed once more.

"It tasted like my mother's apple dumplings; but better. There was some sort of caramel topping on the dumpling. Am I right?" He asked wishing she would touch his lips again. What he really wanted to say to her was please touch me again.

"It is better than your mother's?" She asked delighted with a smile spreading across her face.

"You are definitely one up on my mother. Do I get a whole one? That was really good!"

"Yes!" She stated handing him a plastic fork and the rest of an Apple Dumpling resting in a paper bowl. "I have decided to let Apples be my trademark. The fruit is easy for me to obtain here and at the supermarket in the winter. How does Naomi's Apple Dumpling Delights sound? I wish to have sticker labels made for my breads and other items."

"Draw your sticker logo up, how you want it, and I will make you some stickers on my computer." He replied devouring the apple Dumpling that was indeed just like his mother's, but better.

"What would you want in return?" She asked. Naomi was a barterer.

"Next winter, when we have Saturday afternoons free, I want you to teach me to sew on buttons and mend seams. I have a closet full of shirts with missing buttons and pants with the pocket seams that have come loose." He replied. He did not want to spend another long winter not seeing her. He had thought long and hard for a legitimate reason to see her, even if it meant him cutting all the buttons off of every shirt he owned and undoing his trouser pockets.

"You wish to learn to mend and sew?" She asked with a surprised look on her face.

"After we repair my clothes, I thought I might like you to teach me to quilt. Do you think in one winter's time you could teach me quilting?"

"Where would we meet for this sewing? It cannot be my apartment. Joel is away right now due to being very ill. It would be inappropriate for me to have you in my apartment in his absence."

"We will work that out next winter. Did you say your husband is away?"

"Yes, he is very ill." She replied but did not offer any further explanation.

Marcus was pleased. He did not want to think of her being under the covers with any man but him. He felt guilty, but he was glad her husband Joel was away and guiltily hoped that he did not return.

"It is a deal then, you will teach me to sew next winter?"

"There is a man's quilt called a bow tie. I will draw off the pattern and have it ready for next winter." She replied

A customer walked up snagging Naomi's attention away from Marcus. He stepped back and leaned against his jeep sipping his coffee and wondering where Joel was. He decided that Naomi's ill husband had to be in a nursing home or hospital possibly with a terminal illness. He felt really guilty loving some sick man's wife. His mother would be ashamed of him. That bothered him. For the first time in his life, he felt a respect for his mother's beliefs on marriage. She had tried to instill in him that there was one woman for every man and that marriage was for life. He knew Naomi was that woman, and she was just like his Bible thumping mother. What he didn't know, was what to do about her ill husband.

After a few minutes, the pair resumed their conversation. Naomi had sold a pan of Apple dumplings and a couple loaves of bread.

"I have a problem, Marcus. Could you explain to me how to level my apartment stove so that my breads and cakes bake even. I have been putting butter knives under one end of my baking pan to bake. It is time consuming."

"You need a man to tip your stove and turn the little leveling feet on the bottom of it. I realize your husband is away and ill. How about letting me drop by your apartment one night this week, after I complete my work day, and I will level the feet for you?" He asked seeing an opportunity.

"I will have to stand out on the stairs while you do it. A married Amish woman cannot be alone with a non-husband man. It is forbidden. I know of no one to chaperone and have no children to stand by my side."

"Standing on the stairs sounds reasonable. If my mother had her way, I wouldn't be alone with a woman till my wedding night." He replied grinning.

"Someday, I must meet your mother. I am sure that I will like her very much. She has my values. Do you have someone in mind to marry? If not, your mother and I could arrange a marriage with someone that would not even kiss you till your wedding day." She replied to annoy him. He was always comparing her to his mother. "My husband Joel and I were an arranged marriage. I did not kiss him till the eve of our wedding and then only once."

"Yes, I have a woman that I am seeing once a week, my intended as you say. It is my mother's future reaction that bothers me. She will not find the love of my life acceptable, I am afraid."

"You have a lady friend?" Naomi inquired not smiling. She had never considered that possibility.

"Yes, I do!" He stated throwing his empty paper coffee cup into the rear of his jeep till he could dispose of it properly.

"Why would your mother not accept her? Is she ugly, poor mannered, or possibly older than you?"

"She is the most gorgeous woman that has ever walked on two feet. The problem is that she is married." He replied. "Adultery is a hot topic with my mother."

The conversation was interrupted. Marcus had a customer and turned from Naomi to talk with a couple of back yard green thumbs about his gourd seeds.

Naomi eyeing Marcus, as he talked to his customer, felt a little pang of jealousy. She had never considered that he had a life and a lady friend beyond their Saturdays together. She wasn't sure that she wanted to share him and was embarrassed to find she was possessive of him. She had no right to be. She was married, even if she hadn't seen her husband for almost six years.

Marcus turned back to her after his customers moved on. He was a dark haired, blue eyed, six foot, athletic man wearing jeans and a sports logo hooded sweatshirt. For the first time, Naomi took a really good look at him and gulped. He was magnificent. Her Joel was homely compared to him.

"What is your life like beyond Saturdays?" Naomi asked suddenly wanting to possibly get a hint of what his lady friend was like. "Tell me what I do not know about you . . . and your lady friend. You do know that it is a sin to see a married woman."

"Damn it, Naomi. You sound just like my mother." He replied annoyed that she would preach to him. "I moved here to Paducah to get away from my mother and her 'THOU SHALT NOTS'. Now you are Bible thumping me with them. Don't preach at me!"

"I am sorry. It is indeed none of my business. I have overstepped friendship's boundaries. You have your private life and I mine." She quickly replied seeing his agitated demeanor. She knew that she had really ruffled his feathers. She also knew that she needed to take a step back. Marcus had a lady friend and her attraction to him was not right. She was married till she either obtained a divorce, or Joel was declared dead in the courts.

For a moment, Marcus closed his eyes and didn't respond to her apology. She could see him taking a deep breath. He then opened his eyes and returned to waiting on his customers.

Naomi stepped to the back of her booth. Having no customers, she stared at Marcus' backside. He was a very handsome man and she definitely liked the way his long legs looked in his jeans. They fit just right. However, it was his hands that fascinated her. He had rather large hands with long fingers. She could see his hands holding his lady friend very securely. His lady friend was lucky. Naomi was sure his lady friend never had to sleep in a closet in fear of her nightmares being real. Marcus' hands probably held his lady friend's hands securely in the night and she had no fear of nightmares calling. Naomi was green with envy. She really did not want to think about Marcus in the arms of a married woman somewhere. He had been hers till this morning in her thinking.

Naomi had considered dating him someday, when her divorce was final or Joel declared dead. That dream in her had just died. She was indeed alone with only her letter friends to love her; Molly, Rachael, and Reverend Beecham. Marcus would probably abandon their friendship some day when his married lady friend was divorced or had left her husband for him. The English, like Molly, divorced and left their husbands so easily. Naomi wasn't sure she wanted to be friends with Marcus' lady friend, should she show up at the market and stand with him selling gourd seeds in his booth some day. It was time to step back and take a new look at her life and refocus her attentions.

An unwanted tear rolled down Naomi's cheek. She quickly wiped it away so no one could see. This was not how she expected her new market year to start. She was appalled at herself, as well as angry with Joel for leaving her in a state of limbo. She was not free to love. She was existing in an Amish no –man's land. Joel and his madness had robbed her of six years of being a woman. Her bed and arms had been empty for what seemed like an eternity. Now Marcus, and his words of having a married lady friend, had robbed her of the hope of loving again. She wanted a new life and a man to hold her, and keep her safe. Without Marcus to think and fantasize about, she was alone, so alone. Someone owned Marcus' heart and arms. That she would have to deal with.

The first opening day of the market was extremely busy and there had not been a lot of time for Naomi and Marcus to further talk. Naomi was glad; because she was afraid she might show her jealousy. She needed time to get her emotions in check.

Having sold her last item, Naomi quickly prepared her rolling tote to go home, stuffing her items into it. She wanted out of the market before her emotions burst at the seams and she flooded the place with tears. Her world had been half way tolerable when she had Marcus to fantasize about. Now, her hope and fantasies were gone and all she had left was her mundane work, nightmares, and her attempts to try to create for herself a new Garden of Eden to live in. A Garden of Eden without a companion to share it with, was a desert; not a Garden.

Looking about, she saw that Marcus had walked to the far end of the market to buy vegetables from a friend of his for the week. He had his back to her. She quickly scurried away from the market pulling her rolling tote as fast as it would go. She could not bear to tell Marcus bye for the day, knowing he was possibly heading for the arms of his married woman lover after the market. She was going home, sit in her clothes closet, pull the door shut, and then sit and cry where no one could hear her.

"Why is she pulling her cart so fast?" Frankie Frances asked walking next to Osceola as they followed Naomi, walking behind her.

"She wants to get away quickly from the market and the jackass who sits up next to her." Osceola replied.

"You have a foul mouth for an angel, Osceola. God will get you for it! Last month he took away my chocolate supply for asking my friend, 'What did you do, pop God's suspenders? My friend was on suspension and he would not tell me what for. The word Jackass just might get your chocolate supply taken away. Did you know that I didn't have a pimple one that month! Anyway . . ." she stated not pausing to take a breath. Once you got her started she was a chatterbox. "God may see you as a fallen angel for your use of foul language and send you to Hell, or worse yet take your chocolate." The pony tailed, glasses wearing, wimpy teen stated.

"I am already in Hell and you are one of Satan's imps nipping at me." Osceola retorted in a harsh sticky, syrupy voice. "Girl, you have got to learn to cool your mouth a little. You talk non-stop."

"I am not an imp." The thirteen year old stated biting her lip and tearing up. "God says He will let me in guardian angel school, after I graduate dog walking school, and take a course in communication. He loves me. You, however, are a demoted, foul mouthed, sticky voiced death angel who has been demoted to guarding a white cap that has nothing going on in her life. However, I am trying to be nice so I will tell you that you do have great taste in toe nail polish. I will polish the toenails of the Hounds of Heaven when I get back up there with the same color polish you have on your toe nails. Do you scratch your fleas like the Hounds of Heaven do with their nails?"

"You think you are being nice?" Osceola retorted asking and trying to control herself. Her new mouthy, wimp of an imp, assistant had just insulted the Hell out of her. Guarding the white caps was going to be a long tour of duty with the teen imp in tow."

Stopping in their tracks to argue and bad mouth each other, Osceola and Frankie Frances forgot about Naomi and didn't see her disappear from their sight.

As Naomi was moving along with her rolling tote with her head hung down and about to burst into tears, she heard a male's voice.

"Wait up!"

She turned to see Jack, the vendor who sat up next to Marcus, trying to catch up with her. He was walking as fast as he could. He had abdominal surgery back in the winter, and he was still moving a little awkwardly.

"Have you closed down your vendor booth for the day?" Naomi asked forcing herself to smile as she waited for him.

Jack had stayed with her the previous winter for awhile as he recuperated from surgery. He had no family and Naomi had sat with him in the hospital as well as took him home and nursed him after his hospital stay.

"What are the tears all about, sweet thing? I saw you wipe away that tear earlier at the market, when you thought no one was looking. I won't have my girl going home and crying alone in her closet." He stated taking the handle of her rolling cart from her. "I know you Naomi. I stayed with you for six weeks and there was no TV to pass the time. I spent the days studying your every move, word, prayer and tear. Tell me what is wrong."

"I guess you have got to know me better than anyone. I am sad, Jack. Marcus told me about his lady friend today. For some reason, I never pictured him as having a lover or a girl friend. My life has been so lonely, that I guess I leeched on to him not thinking he had a life beyond me and Saturdays."

"He told you about Jenkins? That surprises me." Jack stated as they walked.

"Is that her name?" Naomi asked with big tears rolling down her cheeks.

Jack stopped pulling the cart and reached out and took her in his arms pulling her to him and resting his chin in the top of her white cap as her flood gate opened.

"I'm sorry! I thought you knew about her. I wouldn't hurt you for any reason, Naomi. Marcus should have told you about her long ago." He stated. "You are my friend and Marcus is my friend. You have to be a toy that he is using to possibly make her jealous and reconsider. They had an affair for about three years, before you came along. She has refused to leave her husband for Marcus, although he has asked her to. Just before you showed up at the market, he asked her to move to California with him. I don't think she was in love with him like he was her. She is a tall, gorgeous, blonde model type who gets off on toying with men. I am sure Marcus was just a toy to her. I am surprised he told you they were seeing each other again. I didn't even know that."

"I have been a fool, Jack. You don't know what it is like to sit alone for five years in an isolated farm house with no one to talk to except an elderly postman once a day. I am like a sponge wanting someone to love me and keep me safe. I mistook Marcus' friendship for possibly more. I am at fault. He has never said anything to make me believe there could be more between us. He has just been friendly and nice to me and I was vulnerable and desperate for a friend, when I first arrived here. I might have embraced any friendly vendor setting up next to me."

"Don't cry; sweet thing. I am really sorry and would never add to your misery."

After a moment or so of tears, Naomi pulled back and started wiping her eyes and nose on the sleeve of her gray Amish dress. She did not have a tissue or handkerchief available.

"I am so lonely, Jack. I spent five, lonely years on the farm waiting for a husband who abandoned me. Now, I am still lonely and in a state of limbo. I am saving my money to get a divorce. However, I cannot have the companionship of a man till I am free. The tenets of my faith are important to me. Marcus and all the vendors have someone to be with on the other days of the week. I do not. I feel like I am in a big, six day, empty box that I cannot get out of and there is no one in the box to share my state of limbo with."

"Well, sweet thing. You have me. I am just as lonely as you are. Since my surgery, I haven't felt it wise to indulge in a relationship that I can't temporarily do anything about. What do you say we run out to the steak house and gorge ourselves eating the biggest steak on their menu? Afterwards, I will help you pin your new quilt into your quilting frame. I am lonely enough to even cut some quilt blocks for you, if you want. Later, when the stars come out, we will sit out on your stairs and listen to the night sounds and the Saturday night blast of Karen's stereo. Then we could take a slow walk down by the river. Slow meaning, I can't walk very fast at the present. You will have to match your pace to mine. You don't have to be alone and I don't have to be alone."

"Thank you, Jack! A steak it is. After we return from the steak house, I will fix you a huge man's dish of apple cobbler with ice cream on top. Instead of cutting quilt blocks, suppose we ask Karen to come up and join us. We could play that card game you were teaching me while you were ill. She is just as lonely as you and I and spends her weekend evenings alone. She is still in love with the sailor, salesman husband who left her."

"Two gorgeous women all to myself for the night . . . I have died and gone to Heaven." He laughed as they started walking toward her apartment to rid them-selves of the rolling tote. "How would you feel, Naomi, if I asked Karen out? I kind of like that wild, red, frizzy hair of hers." He stated not wanting Naomi to know that it was her that he was in love with. Naomi had boundaries and he had figured out a way to get around them. Dating Karen or talking about having been out on a date with someone, threw Naomi off guard. If Naomi felt he was seeing someone, she would not be threatened by him as a man and would let down her fences and do things like go out to the steak house with him. She would not see him as a man wanting to sleep with her or date her before her divorce was final. He understood her and was willing to wait for her to discover him. Karen could be the mask he wore while he waited. At the same time, he would not sleep with Karen or compromise his love for Naomi. He respected Naomi too much. Karen, in love with her ex-husband, would not expect anything from him.

"I am happy for you, Jack. Yes, it is okay with me for you to date my land-lord. She is very nice, except she drinks too many bottles of beer on Saturday nights." Naomi stated grinning. "I do not wish to find you drunk on the stairs below my apartment on the weekends. I expect you to be a man of honor with her." Naomi stated forgetting her tears.

"I would never do anything, Naomi, that would make you ashamed of me or that I would feel guilt at having to tell you. You are my number one girl!" He replied. "Karen is lonely and I am lonely. I think we could be good for each other. However, I actually prefer girls with dark buns who smell like apples."

"Oh, you . . ." She replied. "You are always teasing me. If I was a smart woman, I would prefer a man like you who has recently had surgery and cannot run very fast. I would not have to worry about you abandoning me. If you ran from me, I would just chase you and bring you back. I think the best thing for a runner is to take away their shoes."

"Surgery has taken away my shoes. I am a little slow moving at the moment. Do you think Karen will be okay with a man that is a little slow?"

"She had a runner. I think she is ready for a slower moving man. If she is a smart woman, she will latch on to you and keep you forever chained to her bed. You are a definite keeper."

"So are you, sweet thing." He replied as he helped her up her apartment house steps with her rolling tote. "Do you want to change before we go to the steak house? If you don't mind, I would like to jump in your shower. I sweated like a pig at the market today and I don't smell like your delicious apple pie."

"You shower first and then I will. I think it is probably a good idea that we freshen up a little bit. I do not wish to hang on to the arm of a male skunk at the steak house and I am sure that you do not wish the same hanging on your arm. You may use my toothbrush if you wish, just wash it out thoroughly when you are done."

"I can use your toothbrush?" Jack asked surprised. Sometimes husbands and wives did that in emergencies, but not as a norm.

"You have proven your friendship to me Jack. What is mine is yours."

"You will never know what this moment means to me. What is mine is yours too, Naomi; no questions asked." He replied with tears welling up in his eyes.

CHAPTER TWELVE

Sleeping in The Closet

Marcus returned to his vendor's booth to find that Naomi had packed up for the day and left. "Damn it! Why did you wait so late in the day to go buy freaking vegetables?" He muttered mad at himself. He had intended to ask Naomi to take a walk down by the river. He had blown his chance over some vegetables. He was totally pissed at himself as he loaded up his crates and Naomi's table. There was no way he could go to her apartment and ask her. Her sick husband might be there.

The following work week was never ending, or so it seemed to Marcus. He was desperate to see Naomi. Every day without her presence somehow seemed like an eternity. Leveling her stove was the only legitimate excuse he had for dropping by her apartment. He decided Thursday would be best, because she would start her baking then. Maybe she would lighten up and let him stay and help, even if her husband was there. He was hopeful.

Parking his jeep in front of Naomi's apartment complex, he took a deep breath to calm his jitters and then climbed to the third floor. He hoped that Joel wasn't home from the hospital. It was a crap shoot what would happen when he knocked.

Knocking a couple times on the door, he realized she was not at home. Walking back down the stairs, he spotted the manager's apartment door and decided to inquire if they knew if Naomi would be gone long. He gave a sensible hard knock on the manager's door. It opened revealing a nice looking, red haired woman about his age who had her hair up in one disastrous, wild, red, frizzy ponytail.

"Yes . . ." she greeted him.

"Are you the manager?"

"Yes. I am Karen Cameron, the manager."

"I am Marcus, a friend of Naomi Toombs. I may have knocked on the wrong door. I am not sure. Anyway, I promised to drop by and level her stove legs for her."

"Oh yea . . . ! She has told me about you. Naomi has walked to the super-market for a can of cinnamon. She ran out and needs it for her baking tonight. She will be right back."

"Great!" Marcus replied. "Is her apartment the one at the top of the stairs?"

"Let me grab my keys and I will go up with you to help. I am sure she will return shortly. If not, you can come back down and have a bottle of beer with me till she gets back."

Disappointed that Naomi was not there, he reluctantly climbed the stairs and entered Naomi's apartment with the landlord hot on his heels. Once in the kitchen, he leveled the stove and listened to Karen run at the mouth. She talked non-stop. When he could get in a word here and there, he tried to steer the conversation to Naomi and Joel. Curiously, he couldn't see any signs of a man having ever lived in the apartment.

"Where is Naomi's husband, Joel?" He finally got around to asking as he rose and pushed the stove back into its original position.

"Oh honey, who knows? He walked out on her about five or six years ago. She has not seen him since." Karen replied as Marcus opened the oven door.

"He what . . .?" Marcus asked thinking he had heard wrong.

"She hasn't told you?"

"Told me what?" He asked finishing up by placing a rectangle pan of water in the oven to see if the water in it was level.

"Her husband Joel pushed her down about six years ago and kicked her till she was black and blue. She was seven months pregnant at the time. Her unborn baby, a girl, was severely injured. When it was born thirty minutes later, it lived fifteen minutes in her arms. Due to the isolation of her farm, she never made it to the hospital. She gave birth in her kitchen floor where her jerk of a husband left her. The baby was long dead by the time the paramedics got there. Her husband basically murdered his unborn child. He kicked it to death in her womb."

"Oh God . . . "Marcus muttered. "I did not know."

"That isn't all," Karen replied.

"There is more?" Marcus questioned with a knife in his gut. He had always wanted children and the thought of someone kicking Naomi had him teetering on the edge.

"She had a five year old son whom she had to send to a neighboring farm for help because she was bleeding out and in labor. Her son was a bad asthmatic. The day was rainy and her son caught a cold. He died a week later from complications from Asthma and pneumonia. She lost and buried two children in one week. Her husband Joel walked away leaving her in the floor injured seriously with multiple broken bones and in labor."

"Is he in prison?" Marcus asked thinking that was what Naomi meant when she said he was away.

"She has not heard from him since. He walked away into the morning rain and never returned."

"Wow . . ." Marcus blurted out totally in shock. "The only thing she has ever told me is that her husband is very ill and away."

"She believes her husband is mentally ill, schizophrenic. He walked away from their farm on numerous occasions prior to the day he kicked her. Returning days, weeks, and months later, he would apologize stating he did not know where he had been. Once he disappeared for six months. This time, he has been gone for going on six years."

"So, she is married, but not married." Marcus stated trying to make sense of the situation.

"In her eyes she is married. She is Amish with a strict moral code. The Amish marry till death no matter what with the exception for adultery."

"She is actually free to date me, except that it is her Amish beliefs that are holding her back! My God . . . she is my mother."

"I hope her jackass of a crazy husband gets his taste of what it is like to lose and bury two children alone. Did you know that Naomi sleeps in her clothes closet because of her nightmares? She thinks he will one day return to kick and finish killing her? She has nightmares about it. She says there was a look in his eyes the day he pushed her down and started kicking her. She says she could see in his eyes that he wanted to kill her." Karen stated.

"She sleeps in a closet . . ." Marcus asked in shock. "She sleeps with a butcher knife?"

"Follow me!" Karen stated leading him into the bedroom and opening a closet door for him to take a look. In the closet hung one gray Amish dress that was perfectly pressed. On the floor of the closet was a pallet bed. Beside the pillow on the pallet, lay a flashlight and a butcher knife.

"Oh God . . . Oh God . . . she is afraid!"

"Wouldn't you be, if you had nightmares of your husband pushing you down, kicking the Hell out of your pregnant belly, and then him walking away not helping you? He left her on the floor bleeding out, dying, and giving birth at the same time."

Tears rolled down Marcus' face. He quickly brushed them away. The woman he loved was traumatized and he didn't have a clue as how to help her.

"I am sorry, Karen." He said wiping his tears away. "I must have had my head up my ass to not have seen something was wrong. What am I going to do about this?"

"Would you like to have a beer with me downstairs? I cried myself, when she broke down in the winter and told me about it. Naomi is fragile, Marcus. She is here trying to forget, start over, and put space between her and her nightmares. She does not want anyone to know about Joel or to talk about it. She sees all of us as heathen, basically. If she couldn't trust her Amish husband, down deep she definitely doesn't think she can trust heathen English men. You are lucky to get an apple fritter from her."

"Maybe I will take a beer," He stated following her downstairs shaken to his core.

Reaching the bottom step, his cell phone rang. He quickly answered it in an annoyed voice. It was his sister. She seemed to always call at the most inappropriate moments.

"I am in labor and need you to pick up Adam. Joe is gone to St. Louis. Hospital social services has Adam. I had no one to leave him with." His sister stated.

"You want me to come now?" He asked totally pissed. "Can't you call a neighbor to pick up Adam? I have a serious problem here!" Marcus stated in a harsh voice to his sister who hadn't kept half the babies she had carried. He could count at least four abortions.

"Now, Marcus! My neighbors hate me and Joe has been in St. Louis for some time. We are temporarily split up. I haven't heard from him. Our split up was my fault. I took money he needed for his occupation and bought lottery tickets. If you don't pick Adam up, the hospital will call the welfare and they will snatch him. I can't afford to lose the food stamps and welfare money I get for him. This baby, I am having, will increase the amount of food stamps and other freebies given away here and there. Otherwise, I would have had an abortion. Come get Adam, do your part to help me."

"Damn you Angela. Having kids isn't about using them for freebies and food stamps. You should make arrangements ahead of time for a babysitter for Adam." He shouted. "It is irresponsible not planning ahead. It is irresponsible having kids you do not want."

"Come get Adam, now, Marcus." His sister's voice demanded and then she hung up on him.

Marcus flipped his cell phone closed in disgust.

"I gather you have a family member imposing on your good nature!" Karen stated.

"I have a sister from Hell who lives and breathes to dump her kids on me and suck me dry of whatever she can get out of me." He replied mad. "She thinks having abortions is a form of birth control. I have just about had it with her. She has had four abortions in the last two years." Naomi needed him and he was going to have to go chase after his irresponsible sister. "Will you tell Naomi that I was here and leveled her stove? Tell her I want to have a long talk with her on Saturday."

"Yes, I will tell her. Is there anything else you would like me to tell her?"

"Tell her . . . what do I say, Karen? I am not supposed to know what you have told me."

"You are madly in love with her, aren't you?" Karen smirked asking.

"Yes, but she does not see me or my love for her. Am I unattractive? I am getting a little older and my turning thirty isn't too far off."

"You are one damn good looking man, in my book. If I was Naomi, I would have you upstairs in that closet with me. But, I am not her. She was raised in a prim and proper Amish culture with an extreme set of moral standards that you and I scoff at. She thinks somewhat different than us, due to her background. We cannot force our ways on her or expect her to change because we would like it. If you love her, Marcus, give her space to finish saving her money for a divorce. She won't let any man stick a foot in her door until she feels she is free in God's sight. Also, she may be a little slow in hiring a detective to find him and in suing him for a divorce, because she is afraid to face him in a courtroom. She does sleep with a butcher knife."

"She has definitely kept me at arms' length and now, thanks to you, I understand. Would you be willing to let me drop by on Thursdays on the pretense of seeing you, so I can check on her? That closet thing has me really worried."

"Hey, I am single. A good looking hunk like you can drop by anytime for a beer."

"Thank you, Karen. I just imagine you and I are going to become good Thursday friends while I figure out how to get my foot in her door."

"Probably so . . . What is your occupation, Marcus?"

"I am a professor at the university in the agriculture and science departments. Botany and the growing of exotic plants are my passion. For the last few years, I have been experimenting with crossing gourd varieties."

"Well, at least we have something in common. I am a fourth grade elementary teacher. However, I have no green thumb and I will have to leave the exotic gourd growing up to you."

"I really appreciate your telling me about Naomi." Marcus stated pausing and then added. "I have got to drive to Nashville to pick up my sister's kids. I don't have any choice in the matter. May I have a rain check on that beer?"

"You've got it. Be safe and see you next Thursday."

Marcus and Karen did not see invisible Osceola and Frankie Frances hanging out with them. Osceola didn't follow Naomi around every moment of the day. A tracking device in her nail file warned her if anything was going wrong in Naomi's world. She had put a tracking chip in the heel of Naomi's old lady, black shoes the night she slept on the hay bale. Heaven was a place of extremely advanced technology. After all, God was the great inventor who sometimes gave his ideas to men on Earth to create and manufacturer. However, all technological thought came from God the great inventor. He was a brilliant White Suit, but sometimes was a butt face when being a boss, in Osceola's opinion.

Listening to Marcus and Karen was sort of like listening in on a private telephone conversation. A little gossip never hurt anyone and she and Frankie Frances were bored to tears. Their white cap never got into trouble or caused trouble. The only thing they ever did for her was dry tears. Any three year old angel could do that for her.

"His sister has had four abortions?" Frankie Frances asked in shock turning to look at Osceola.

"Actually, the number is seven." Osceola replied. "I came for all seven of their little souls over the past few years. I am a death angel."

"Didn't their father try to stop her?" A big eyed Frankie Frances asked.

"None of them had the same father and all were conceived on one night stands!" Naomi stated not wanting to have to explain about prostitutes and Johns.

"Is Marcus' sister a . . . you know?" Frankie Frances asked not wanting to say the word whore.

"Honey, you might as well get used to humans doing the unthinkable. If you accompany me on the rest of my mission, you are definitely going to get your birds and bees education." Osceola replied in her sticky, syrupy, sweet fly catching voice. "Do you have a little, pimple faced boyfriend in Heaven that you are sweet on?"

"Do you have an unsuspecting, long legged fly hidden out up north that you have caught with your fly paper tongue?" Frankie Frances shot back.

Osceola looked at her. She was not used to having another female angel get in her face and shoot down her words. She asked herself what she had done to deserve being stuck with a teen version of herself. The only difference between the two of them was that she was black and Frankie Frances was white. If she didn't know better, the kid could be hers and that was not a pleasant thought.

CHAPTER THIRTEEN

THE BOY GUTTER RAT

Saturday arrived once more. Naomi was pleased that Marcus had leveled her stove. It had made her last two evenings of baking much easier. She could hardly wait to see him and thank him for his effort in doing so. Spending time with Jack had taken the edge off of her loneliness. She was sure she now had a grip on her jealousy and her feelings for Marcus.

Naomi kept telling herself that Marcus, like Jack, had a right to have a lady friend. They were single and she was not. She would try to act normal, sell her breads and jellies, and further enjoy their friendship for what it was. She had told herself firmly that she was not falling in love with Marcus. Her feelings for him were just caused by her having no one else to talk to and she would attempt to make more friends. Marcus was a friend and she would make more like him. In her thinking, she had limited herself on Saturdays.

Nearing her market spot, she wondered why he had not run to meet her as he usually did. As she entered the farmer's market building, she saw that a child was talking with him. He had probably gotten distracted and hadn't seen her coming. It was a little boy speaking with Marcus. The youth had his back to her. From behind, she was shocked to see that he looked amazingly like her dead son, Adam. A flood of painful memories swept over her. She swallowed to keep from crying. She didn't want Marcus or any of the vendors to see her shed tears or know about her other life. She was not at the market for sympathy. The market was her new life.

Approaching her card table, she smiled at Marcus who was grinning from ear to ear. Then she watched as Marcus put his hands on the little boy's shoulders and turned him around to face her. Naomi, in instant shock, dropped everything in her hands and gasped with her mouth falling open. It was her son, Adam.

"Naomi, I have someone I want you to meet," Marcus stated in an excited voice.

Naomi was speechless. It was Adam her son. Then she quickly told herself it couldn't be because her son would be eleven going on twelve now. The Adam standing in front of her was younger. Plus, her son was dead and buried in a rural farm cemetery back in Missouri. How could this be? Was she seeing things? Had her mind snapped from the emotional stress she had endured?

"Who is he?" Naomi managed to blurt out asking.

"This big man is my nephew, Adam."

"His name is Adam?" She questioned big eyed and not smiling. Her son had been named Adam. Joel named him.

"He is the son of my sister who lives in Nashville. He has come to stay with me for a short spell. His mother is in the hospital giving birth to a baby sister."

"A baby sister?" Naomi managed to spit out asking in spite of her shock.

"Angela my sister and her boyfriend, Joe, plan to name this big boy's new sister, Martha."

Naomi reached for the edge of her card table to steady herself. She had instant jelly for knees. Martha was her mother-in-law's first name.

"He is your sister's son?" She managed to ask repeating what he had said.

"Yes, he belongs to my sister, Angela. I drove to Nashville Thursday evening after leveling your stove to pick him and his sister Mary up. Adam's dad and my sister had a little spat and split up. She needed me to watch Adam and Mary till she is settled in with her new baby, Martha."

"How old are her children?" Naomi managed to ask eyeing Adam. He was the spitting image of her dead son, but didn't appear to have the asthmatic symptoms her Adam had shown. The pollens and smells from the items at the market would have set her son into a coughing, choking frenzy.

"Adam is eight and his sister Mary is seven. I hope to introduce you to her sometime this week. I left her with a sitter for the morning. She had a little bit of a runny nose and I thought the market air might complicate her problem. She has asthma. I have to be careful with her."

"He has a sister named Mary who is seven and she has asthma?" She asked counting in her head. If this Adam and Mary belonged to her Joel, Marcus's sister Angela had to be pregnant with both of them during the time she lived on the farm with Joel. Was it possible that Joel had a second family that he wandered away to and then returned lying to her about not knowing where he had been? Had he caused the death of her children to embrace those of another?" She kept holding to the table as her soul trembled and her knees shook.

Naomi took a close look at the boy's face. He had an identical mole on his left cheek to that of her son, Adam. Her son's mole was identical to her father-in-law's mole on his left cheek. Now there was a third male with the same identical mark. There were too many coincidences. Naomi was shaken to her core, but didn't dare speak of her suspicions to Marcus. She did not want anyone knowing about her former life.

"Act normal Naomi," She muttered to herself. Ask questions and get as much information as you can from Marcus and the boy. If Joel is out there and alive, this may be God's way of showing you where he is and that he is an adulterer. If the boy's father is Joel, you have the right to a divorce because he is living with a second woman and he is not crazy. He left you on purpose each time making his way to them. By telling you he had amnesia, he could come back to you, his parents, and the Amish community whenever he wanted.

"So, where did you say his sister, Mary is?" She asked forcing herself to smile.

"I dropped her off at day care, because she has a runny nose. The big man here will be more than happy to play behind our booths with the little car I bought him on the way over."

"How old did you say Mary is?" Naomi asked wanting to get her facts straight.

"My sister is seven, dumb ass. Do you have dirt in your ears?" Adam piped up.

"Adam . . ." Marcus retorted loudly in shock. "That was not nice!"

"Forget her, Uncle Marcus. She is not worth wasting our morning on. She is just a stupid, dumb broad who is wearing an ugly, outdated gray dress. She isn't pretty like Jenkins."

"Adam . . . you will not say another word. Get up in my jeep and stay there till I tell you to get down. You hear me?" Marcus stated pointing to the jeep. Adam put his fingers in his ears and waved them at Naomi as he went.

"I am so sorry, Naomi." Marcus stated in total humiliation. The last thing he wanted was her to find out about his married lover that he had broken up with just before meeting her.

"It should be him saying that he is sorry, not you!" She replied and turned to wait on a customer. The morning got busy and it was noon before they had a chance to take a break. Adam got down out of the jeep and did play behind their two booths with his little car. However, Naomi ignored him except for an occasional glance at the mole on his face, when he was not looking.

"Wow . . ." Marcus stated turning to her. "This has been one busy morning."

"Yes, it has been." Naomi replied trying to remain calm and collected to gain what information she needed. "What is Adam's last name?"

Adam piped up from behind her, "My name is Adam Too!"

"Too . . .?" Naomi asked turning to Marcus thinking she had misunderstood him. As she asked, she shocked herself by suddenly realizing that Joel could have dropped the last letters of their last name making it Too.

"I know that it is an unusual last name." Marcus replied. "I never heard it either till Angela introduced him to me. I questioned my sister about the name when she first met him. He claims to be from distant oriental ancestry and that is where he gets his name." Marcus stated softly so Adam could not hear as he rolled his eyes.

"How did your sister meet him?" She asked digging for all she could get.

"He was a hitchhiker that was traveling down the highway by my home place. My sister, who was fifteen and had just got off the school bus, sat down to talk with him on the side of the road. They just walked away down the road with neither one of them looking back. We thought Angela was dead. We found her book bag up by the highway. She called back home, after she turned eighteen. My sister does not have a lick of sense or feelings for others and how what she does affects them. My mother almost lost it thinking she had been kidnapped and murdered. She and the hitchhiker, Joe, ended up in Nashville. My sister is still there, but Joe has left her and moved to St. Louis from what Angela told me when I went to pick Adam up. She hasn't seen him in several months."

"What did the hitchhiker look like?" Naomi asked wanting to hear him say that he was Amish.

"We never saw or met him till after she turned eighteen. He is a tattoo freak now. His body is covered with them, including half of his face. I don't know what he looked like back then." He replied turning to check to see if Adam was listening. He was busy with his toy car.

"Does her hitchhiker leave her regularly? Karen tells me her husband did. He was a salesman."

"I try not to waste my time on Angela and Joe and their numerous break-ups. He always comes wandering back and they make up. Personally, I think he returns when he is broke and needs her welfare check to survive on. I gave up trying to fix their relationship problems years ago. They are what they are." He replied pausing for a moment. "Don't hold Adam's mouth against me, Naomi. He will be spending a few days with me and then I will take him back home as soon as Angela gets out of the hospital and gets settled. He speaks what he hears. He uses the language and expressions my sister and Joe have taught him. I can't do anything about his way of expressing himself."

"My son, at that age, was saying grace and speaking appropriately in public. Your nephew has had no discipline and is, in my book, a little English heathen!"

Marcus bit his tongue. His day was not turning out as he had planned. Adam had ruined it for him and there was nothing that he could do about it. At the same time, he was a little irked that Naomi would infer that his nephew was less than perfect, a little heathen. He didn't comment on her remark. They both turned to wait on customers for a short while. Then it slowed again.

"Would you mind watching him for a moment while I run get him something from the snack shack to eat to hold him over till we leave here?"

"I am sorry, Marcus, I do not feel obligated to the child as you do. He is mouthy and disrespectful. Take him with you. I owe him nothing."

"Come on, Adam, you are going with me! Naomi will watch your little car while we are gone." He stated with a hint of anger in his voice.

"Take the car with you. It is not mine to watch." She replied and returned to her table where a customer had walked up.

There was no way she was going to do any favors for a child that her husband had possibly replaced hers with. She loved her son too much to disrespect him that way, although she could not tell Marcus why she was not embracing his nephew. She had a pang of sadness sweep over her. She knew that her friendship with Marcus would be coming to an end if his sister's Joe Too was her Joel Toombs. It was time to hire an attorney and a detective. She would double bolt her closet door when she did, so she could continue to sleep.

Marcus returned and Adam was carrying a bag of potato chips and a can of soda. There were no customers at the moment, so, Naomi sat down in her folding chair and took out a cheese and bread sandwich she had made herself for lunch. Being polite, she asked. "Would you Marcus or Adam like half of my cheese sandwich?" She was just trying to appear polite and get thru the day.

Adam piped up, "I don't eat cheap ass, cheese sandwiches. My daddy says he ate that type of crap back on his Missouri farm. We are not cheap ass cheese sandwich eaters and you can take your homemade bread and throw it out to the pigs. My daddy and I get food stamps and we eat the good stuff."

"Adam . . ." Marcus yelled trying to get him to shut up. The last thing he wanted was Naomi to think that his family was welfare trash. He wanted her to love him, not think of him and his family as gutter rats, which was the way Adam was coming across.

"She is a cheap ass bread baker, Uncle Marcus. My dad hates cheese and plain women. You should too!"

"Get in the jeep, Adam. I am taking you home!"

Turning to Naomi with a red face, he stated firmly, "I am really sorry Naomi. My sister has not raised him well and he has picked up on their foul language and preferences. I am really sorry for the way he spoke to you."

"It would be him apologizing, if he were mine. You have condoned his behavior all morning letting him get by with his disrespect. It is not only his sister and father that have made him the way he is. You have failed to discipline him this morning and have had an equal hand in his lack of manners and proper language. Blame yourself, Marcus. You are his guardian and disciplinarian for the moment. I would have taken him over my knee the first time he disrespected an elder or a woman. Afterward, I would have washed his mouth out with soap for his foul language."

"Get in the jeep now!" Marcus stated in a foul mood. He was mad at Adam for ruining his day with Naomi and at her for suggesting that he had made Adam what he was. He had hoped that the three of them would have a nice day together and that Naomi would bond with him. He knew that one day Angela would lose Adam and his sister to the welfare system. He also knew that it would be up to him to step up to the plate and adopt Adam and his sisters. Adam had now alienated the woman he was in love with and down deep wanted to marry.

After Marcus and Adam left, Naomi sat down in her folding chair aghast. She was positive that she had found Joel. Her in-laws were dairy farmers and made their own cheese. It wasn't uncommon for them to eat cheese sandwiches for lunch four or five days a week. Adam's reference to her cheap ass cheese sandwich and his daddy's life on a Missouri farm was the bit of information she needed to move forward in her thinking and do what needed to be done. There was now no doubt in her mind that Joe Too was Joel Toombs.

Naomi was thankful to God for his weaving of the strands of her life. It was not by chance that she had ended up in Paducah. It was part of God's great master plan to avenge her and bring Joel to his knees. Molly, Rachael, Reverend Beecham, Corky, Karen, and Marcus had all been puzzle pieces that God had brought together to bring her justice for her two dead children. She understood now her attraction to Marcus. He was a puzzle piece. It was also okay to put the puzzle pieces away once the puzzle pieces had all been put together.

Rising from her chair, she quickly loaded up her wares. She had to go home, read her Bible, give thanks to God for guiding her path, and then decide what her next step puzzle piece should be. She needed thinking time. Quickly she stepped over to Jack's vendor booth the other side of Marcus'.

"Do you have time later to drop by my apartment? I have something serious I need to discuss with someone, and you are the only person I trust to vent to." She stated and then leaned over and whispered to him. "I may have found Joel. I need to sue him quickly for a divorce before he disappears again. I am going home to think. I could sure use some advice."

"Go ahead and get out of here before Marcus returns. I will be there in about thirty minutes after I break down your display and mine. This is good news, Sweet Thing. I will do anything I can to help you." He whispered back to her.

"Thank you, Jack. Do not tell Marcus or anyone."

"You can trust me. You are my number one girl, remember?"

Thirty minutes before closing, Marcus returned to the Farmers market to find that Naomi was already gone as was his vendor friend Jack on the other side of him. He had brought Adam back to make him apologize. It was too late. He wondered if Naomi would believe him next week if he told her that he did bring his nephew back to make him say he was sorry. He wanted to drive over to her apartment and make it right. However, he had Adam in tow and he was afraid his nephew might say or pull something else that could make Naomi's opinion of him worse.

Extremely pissed barely described how he felt at his sister Angela for throwing Adam as a monkey wrench into his relationship with Naomi. He knew she was the only woman he would ever love, that special someone that comes along once in a life time. Angela, thru Adam, had alienated her and stolen his moment and day with her that could not be replaced.

Osceola Black Lightning and Frankie Frances strolled down thru the center aisle of the farmer's market smelling different vendor's fruits, vegetables, and flowers. Osceola had intended to go down to the river for the afternoon and skip a few stones with her young protégé who was as bored with her assignment as she was. Suddenly, she noticed that Naomi was gone. Grabbing Frankie Francis by the arm, she pulled her in front of Marcus' booth, seeing that he had a strange, pissed off expression on his face. She also saw a little boy standing in the gourd booth with a smirk on his face and darkness in his eyes. She raised her nail file to eye level recognizing the darkness. The child's body was human, but the being inside was not. Marcus continued with what he was doing, because Osceola and Frankie Frances were not visible to the human eye.

"Why do you have your sword pulled?" Frankie Frances asked pushing her slid glasses back up her nose where they belonged. "Is there danger?"

"Girl, you are hopeless and wouldn't recognize darkness and danger if you saw it. Of course there is darkness. Pull your sword and be quick about it. A demon from the pit of Hell has escaped and is hiding in that boy behind Marcus. We have to get him before he gets Naomi. He has come for her. She is a threat to his existence."

"That child has a devil spirit in him!" Frankie Frances asked big eyed having never seen one before.

"Yes, Frankie, pull your sword and prepare for battle if you want to live to see the day you enter guardian school."

Frankie Frances quickly pulled her four inch nail file from her pocket and held it at eye level imitating Osceola. With the other hand she once again pushed her glasses up her nose to where they belonged. She definitely had a problem with her eye wear. However, it was better that your eye glasses slid down, rather than your socks.

"I'm ready, Osceola. He doesn't look dangerous. I think I could take him out by throwing one vial of pimple cream at him."

"This is your chance to prove yourself, Frankie Frances. Strut your stuff and show me what you've got." Osceola replied keeping her sword nail file pointed at the boy.

Frankie Frances planted her feet about eighteen inches apart and bent her knees to do battle. As she did, her glasses once more slid down her nose. Then she yelled, "Take this you demon from the pit. I am Frankie Frances and I am your worst nightmare." Then she gave a little swish and a sway with her file sword, confident that the demon was going to be covered with pimple cream with mint and eucalyptus in it. Demons hated anything cool. The fire pit was their home.

Marcus, not realizing that a war in the Heavens was going on, stepped between Frankie Frances and his nephew Adam oblivious to what was happening. He was just breaking down his gourd and seed display preparing to leave. Suddenly, a big glob of white goo fell covering his head and shoulders.

"What the hell?" He asked in shock as his nephew started laughing and pointing.

"That was one big do-do bird that flew over you, Uncle Marcus. You are covered in white crap."

Marcus was stunned. The bird crap smelled strangely like Mint and Eucalyptus. He then pulled his soaked shirt off and started wiping the goo out of his hair and off of his face.

"Well, girl . . . you did hit a target. I will give you credit for that. However, it was the wrong one. You were supposed to be aiming at the demon."

"My glasses slipped down and caused my aim to be off. It is not my fault." Frankie Frances stated starting to cry. "You don't like me."

"Shut the bawling up. I don't have time for it." Osceola stated shaking her head and rolling her eyes. "When I get you back to Naomi's apartment, I am going to cut a piece of her elastic banding and tie it on your glasses so they won't slip. Your mother should have taken care of your glasses problem long ago."

"Leave my mother out of this, you mean old death angel. I would tell you I hate you, but that wouldn't be nice. So all I am going to say is that you stink."

Frankie Frances stated and quickly swished her small nail file at Osceola and a skunk was beneath her feet spraying her gold stilettos.

Instantly, Osceola began to gag and jump up and down trying to get away from the skunk that was doing its number on her gold stilettos and legs.

Frankie Frances laughed watching Osceola jump and try to get away from the skunk forgetting about the demon in the boy.

"Look Uncle Marcus, a skunk!" Adam Too yelled getting his attention.

"Run, Adam, get in the jeep before it sprays you." Marcus yelled seeing that the skunk was within three feet of them and the gourd booth. Vendors and customers were running from the market because the skunk seemed to be crazed and was running this way and then that way spraying everything in sight.

Frankie Frances had transported a real skunk into the market with her nail file sword. It could be seen, but her and Osceola could not be.

"Get it off of me, get it away from me . . ." Osceola yelled in a panic in her syrupy, sticky, southern twang voice. "Now, Frankie Frances, if you don't want me to tell God how you failed to get that demon. You will be a dog walker forever if he finds out."

"Oh . . ." Frankie Frances stated. "I didn't think about that."

She quickly looked around for the boy with the dark one in him. It was too late. He was nowhere in sight. She quickly swished her nail file and got rid of the skunk and then stood eyeing Osceola who had rage in her eyes and was smelling hideous. Frankie Frances took two fingers and held her nose and faked a smile from ear to ear.

"Sorry about your stilettos." She stated pushing her slid glasses up her nose with her free hand.

"We are here to guard Naomi, not pull teen age pranks. That demon and several others like him are walking about here in human forms. Naomi is their target you little pimple faced piece of dog walking angel crap. You let the demon get away and now I will have to face him another day, not to mention my ruined shoes, hose, and gown." Osceola yelled as the teen angel trembled, shielded herself with her arms, and crouched in fear. She knew she was going to get the grounding of all groundings.

"Hand it over . . ." Osceola demanded putting out her hand.

"Hand what over?" Frankie Frances asked smiling a fake smile from ear to ear and displaying all of her teeth.

"Your sword, you little fool. You used it on the innocent. It is designed to do battle with the Devil in case you don't remember. Now hand it over."

"No . . . it is my nail file. I am nothing without it."

Osceola swished her nail file sword at Frankie Frances. Instantly the nail file flew from the hand of Frankie Frances to the hand of Osceola who being mad melted it into pot metal in the palm of her hand. "From this day forward, while you are my assistant, your duties will consist of shining my gold stilettos. I am demoting you to a shoe shine boy."

Instantly, a booming male's voice sounded above the pair of angels. "I wish I had thought of that one! Shoe shine boy it is. I will assign her to the angel barracks when she gets back up here. They should have enough shoes to keep her busy and out of trouble."

Osceola forgot her anger and grinned from ear to ear. "I'm good."

Then Frankie Frances began to wail and cry. Those at the market, not being able to see her, did not know what was up and thought her wailing sound was tornado winds. A ferocious storm blew up instantly turning the sky greenish black. Then there was thunder, black lightning, and sounds like the booms of canons over head. Sheets of heavy rain blew in and drenched the inside of the market as well as those running for their cars in fear, thinking they and the market were going to be blown away.

When angels cry, storms follow.

"Hush up, Frankie Frances. Do you want the river to over flow its banks. You are crying enough rain to flood the town. You don't want Naomi to drown do you?"

"Oh . . . no . . . that wouldn't be nice, would it?" Frankie Frances stated and immediately stopped crying. "When we get back up to Heaven, I am going to tell Mrs. God on you for destroying my nail file. How do you expect me to grow up and be well groomed like you, if I don't have a nail file? Would you want Mrs. God taking away your toe nail polish for a little bitty bad thing you did?"

Osceola shook her head and rolled her eyes as Frankie Frances followed her out of the market running her mouth. The girl was a chatterbox and never learned. The next time she prayed for a companion, someone to talk with at night, she was going to be more specific in her request and definitely ask for a male. At least they could handle their swords when it was time to do battle. Then she scolded herself. She should have zapped that little demon in that boy and forgot about giving Frankie a chance to prove herself. She had to face it. The girl, that she was somewhat getting attached to, would probably always be a shoe shine boy or a dog walker. Frankie Frances just didn't have what it took to be a guardian or a death angel. She was the type of kid who flunked kindergarten five years in a row.

As they walked out of the market, Osceola took a deep breath and waded into a new conversation with her in an effort to help her.

"Now Frankie Frances . . . not all little girls grow up to be guardian angels, just like not every little Earth human girl grows up to be a movie star. It is okay to fill in and do less gifted positions available in Heaven. On Earth, little boys sometimes play Indians. Not all of them can be medicine men and chiefs. There has to be the ordinary ones who ride ponies and then hold the reins of the horses while the others are sneaking up on the enemy with their knives which we call swords. It is okay to be a rein holder. Someone has to do it."

"Are you jealous because I am more gifted than you?" Frankie Frances asked pushing her glasses up.

"You more gifted than me . . . ?" Osceola questioned in a huff, being taken off guard.

"You did get demoted from death angel status to guardian angel status. I am sorry you just didn't cut it. It is hard when you find out you can't be what God expects you to be. I am sorry you were a failure as a death angel, Osceola. However, you shouldn't take it out on me. I am innocent and doing my best to be nice to you and have empathy. You like to point your finger at me and try to insinuate I am a failure. When you do, you are just trying to make yourself look good in God's eyes. I understand."

"No wonder God made you a dog walker. You are so full of yourself that only a dog could get along with you. You are the failure, Frankie Frances, not me. You are a walking disaster."

Frankie Frances began to tear up and sniffle. "No wonder God is sending you off, when we get back, to guard the Eastern Gate. He must be trying to get you and your syrupy, sticky, fly killing voice out of his presence. Just like humans have white trash, you are Heaven's angel trash? I may be a dog walker, but you are below me on the angel totem pole. I am somebody and I know it. You are so untalented that you couldn't even put a dog leash on your northern long legged Jack Rabbit and keep him. He got a way didn't he?"

"You little witch . . ." Osceola Black Lightning muttered mad as a hornet. "Anymore disrespect out of your mouth and I am going to pop every pimple on your face and then make it break out in hives, boils, and blisters all at the same time. I am a death angel and volunteered for this mission. I deliver souls to hell that are higher class than you. Mess with me and you will get a taste of my gift. I lock and unlock Hell and I can make the elastic go bad in your school girl socks and underwear; not to mention permanently flattening your chest till you will never fill out a camisole."

Frankie Frances broke out into tears and wailing again. Osceola stuck her fingers in her ears to keep from having to listen.

"Osceola . . ." A booming familiar male voice called from Heaven.

"Yes God . . ." Osceola answered forcing herself to smile and answer in her stickiest, syrupy, sweetest southern voice.

"Shut that Frankie Frances kid up. She is driving me crazy. Stick a pacifier in her mouth or a chocolate bar if you have one. Do something!"

"Drive you crazy . . . It is me that she is sending over the edge." Osceola yelled up at God in a loud syrupy, sticky, angry voice. "Take her back!"

"No returns!" God yelled back and then He made the Heavens thunder and black lightning flash.

"He is a little edgy today." Osceola muttered as she grabbed Frankie Frances and started running with her to get her and her wails out of God's hearing range.

CHAPTER FOURTEEN

Naomi Seeks Revenge

The weekend dragged by after Naomi discussed with Jack her options. He was as shocked as she was when she told him her suspicions about Adam Too and Marcus's sister's tattoo man. Jack agreed with her that she had probably stumbled onto her ex and helped her make a phone call and make an appointment with Dan Maynard.

New crushing thoughts plagued Naomi. If Joe Too was her husband Joel Toombs and her vendor friend's nephew Adam was his son, it meant that her husband had never loved her and she had been a fool. He was not crazy the day he kicked her unmercifully and walked away in the rain. He had pushed her down on purpose knowing she was seven months pregnant. He had abandoned his two children and played crazy so he would not have to ever explain his actions to her, his parents, or the community should he want to return. She had been violently used. The male disease, he had brought home to her, had been obtained from Marcus' harlot sister.

Naomi was faced with a new fear which had her nerves on edge. She feared that she would not be able to bring Joel to his knees and justice before he disappeared again. Her children deserved to be avenged. She loved them, even if their father had not. He had purposely tried to kick Mary to death in her womb.

On Monday, after much prayer, Naomi walked to her appointment with

Dan Maynard, the attorney who was Rev. Beecham's nephew. She took her cash savings with her to pay for his services. She knew nothing about banks and had kept her money hidden in a sock in her closet. Once in the lawyer's office, she reiterated her story of her two dead children, her husband's disappearance, and her accidental meeting of a boy named Adam Too who looked just like her dead son including an identical mole on his face. The nicely dressed attorney, a few years older than her, took down all of her information making notes as she spoke. She was careful to include the cheese farm remark and the similarity of names of her children and those of Angela.

"That is quite a story. It is just crazy enough to be believable, Mrs. Toombs." He stated pausing to tap his pencil on his desk for a moment or so deep in thought. "Alright, I think I have all the facts on paper and in my head. Am I correct, you want your husband served with divorce papers in St. Louis where he is currently engaged in a new relationship having just broke up with Marcus' sister. Also, you want him charged with polygamy, if he has married a second time?"

"Yes! I was shunned by my community because of him. I want his shame publicized in the newspapers, so I can send the papers back to everyone in my community shaming them for abandoning me in my time of stress and grief."

"If the man in St. Louis, named Joe Too, is not your husband, you then want to proceed and have him declared dead in the courts so you can go on with your life. Is that correct?"

"Yes. That is correct. However, I feel my God has led me here and Marcus' common law brother-in-law is my missing husband."

"How do you feel about Joe Too if he turns out to indeed be your husband Joel Toombs?"

"It is unfathomable to me that he would abandon my two children never looking back. To name bastard children with the names of your legitimate children is disrespect. To let me cry and wait for five years is disrespect. For him to bring home male diseases to me is disrespect. I forgave him the disease thing because he played crazy and claimed to have amnesia. His lies and using of me were unnecessary. If he did not want to be with me, he should have been a man and told me. In my Amish community, a male must join the church and marry at eighteen. Our marriage was arranged by the brethren, although

133

Joel always told me he fell in love with me after we were married. I was young, naïve, and believed him. He had to marry to be in good standing in our community. It is our way. I was but a pawn in a dark game of deceit and adultery played by him. I want vindication."

"I am sorry that your husband was such a dark, deceitful man. You are an exceptionally beautiful Amish woman. In my thinking, your husband is and was a fool."

Naomi blushed. "Beauty is only skin deep, Mr. Maynard. My Joel was one of the handsomest men in our Amish Community. I was an orphan and felt really special when he married me. I loved him deeply and clung to him because I had no family to love. I have learned to look inside people and not on the outside. In return, I want people to look inside me and see me for who I am and not what my physical body looks like. I did not take the time to look inside Joel when we were courting. He was handsome and I was pleased with his beauty."

"We all have had our moments when others have taken advantage of us. What it does is make a smarter person out of us. You have started a successful baking business and started over with two dresses and a grocery store tote of personal items. You are one smart cookie and a good looking woman that the average man dreams about having on his arm. Good things are waiting for you in your future. Let them happen. I will see to it that your abuser gets what is coming to him."

"Thank you, Mr. Maynard. I appreciate your kind words. How soon will I hear whether Joe Too in St. Louis is my husband?"

"Everyone here knows Marcus. He is a popular professor at a Private University just north of us. Tracing his sister will be no problem. I know Professor Jenkins and she will probably be more than glad to give me any personal information I need in exchange for not telling her husband about her three year affair with Marcus."

"Marcus is a college professor?" Naomi asked in shock.

"Yes. His female students adore him and chase him relentlessly. My sister Mavis has dated him occasionally, over the years. She also teaches at the college. Just about every single professional woman in Paducah has been out with him, at one time or another. He is a lady's man who has a track record of liking married women. He is what you call a non- committer. A married woman doesn't expect him to give up his bachelorhood, so he sees her as a safe roll in the hay."

"I see. He has never mentioned to me that he is a professor. I see that he has not shared his life beyond Saturdays with me."

Naomi was glad that she had kept her emotions intact. She wondered if Marcus had intended for her to be one more roll in the hay to add to his track record. She had been a fool befriending him or thinking any nice looking man would want her. She was ugly. Her husband hadn't wanted her and Marcus had a roll in the hay agenda planned for befriending her.

"Back to Joe Too . . . when will I hear something from you?" Naomi asked.

"After you leave, I will put in a call to Professor Jenkins and ask her to meet me for lunch where I will present her options, for helping us, to her. I will not divulge your name, just in case she runs to Marcus. Then a couple of hours of detective work on my computer and we will come up with an address for Marcus' sister and then Joel in St. Louis. I will tell Angela that her Joe has won a hundred dollars in a supermarket sweepstakes. She will fall all over herself coming up with an address for him, if she thinks she is going to get to keep half. If she divulges an address for her Joe, I then will mail a hundred dollar money order to her saying it is his winnings so she doesn't get suspicious. A hundred dollars is a lot of money to a sewer rat. Next, I will send a detective friend of mine to Nashville and St. Louis seeing what he can dig up visiting the two addresses. He will photograph Angela, her common law husband Joe, their children, place of residence, where he works, his new woman, in St. Louis, etc. I should have the photos for you to look at by next Monday. Then, you can return here to the office, look at them, and tell me for sure whether the man is or isn't your husband. We will then proceed with a divorce or declaring him dead at that point."

"It will be a long week waiting for next Monday." Naomi replied.

"Be prepared! It will be much longer than a week of waiting, Mrs. Toombs. I am guessing it will take a year to get my case together as well as coordinate it with the arrest of your husband; if the man in St. Louis is who you think it is. Because you are charging your husband with adultery, I need you to stay clear of Marcus or any other man. You said your Amish in-laws have money. They will fight us possibly in the courts to save their son's reputation. You have just told me how your mother-in-law got you shunned. We don't want to give them the slightest hint that you are remotely seeing any one, even on a friendship basis. I would prefer that you abandon your booth next to Marcus at the market should the man in St. Louis prove to be your Joel. Also, I would prefer that you not speak to anyone about your friendship with my uncle, the Reverend Beecham. A man is a man, no matter what his age in the courts. We do not want to give your husband or his parents any ammunition for their possible case. I will ask the court to award you the farm, half of any inheritance he may one day receive, and half of all assets he now owns. You are his legal wife. If he is married to Marcus's sister or the woman in St. Louis, I will also see that he is charged with polygamy. You must walk a strict, narrow path for the next year. Do you understand what I am trying to say?"

"Yes, I am to be found blameless and man-less when my court date comes. Lady friends are to be my only companions and my letter writing to your uncle is to be kept a secret. I also must walk away from my friendship with Marcus, if his sister is a wife of my Joel."

"Very nicely put, Naomi. You are a smart woman and at the end of a year, you and your children will be getting justice."

"That is what I want. I want my children's deaths to be avenged. They died for no reason except the selfishness of my husband. There is not a doubt in my mind that the man called Joe Too is my Joel. I want him brought to justice. I want him to pay."

"Unlike you, Mrs. Toombs, I deal in facts. I want to get the detective's findings back, before I proceed any further in my thinking. For the next week, I just want you to keep your lips zipped and tell no one that you have consulted me for any reason."

"I understand. However, I do feel bad for Marcus. We are friends."

"Blood is thicker than water, Mrs. Toombs. Marcus will take his sister's side when the . . . hits the fan!" He stated catching himself just in time to keep from using foul words in front of her.

"My own husband betrayed me, why shouldn't Marcus. What is next, Mr.

Maynard?"

"Don't change your routine except for the dropping of housecleaning for any single man. Don't trust anyone with any detail of what we have spoken of, except Jack. Your friend Jack is an ex-cop. He will keep your confidence. Next Monday, we will decide how to proceed after looking at what my detective can dig up."

"I will do as you say." Naomi replied.

"You are looking at least a year either way you go. If Joel is alive, we have to collect evidence against him as well as work with court procedures and court dates. Then we have process servers to wait on and our case of adultery to be air tight. Can you keep our secrets that long?"

"Yes, Mr. Maynard. I grieved for my dead children for five years alone. I waited for Joel to come home for five years alone. I will gladly bear a year of silence to see Joel pay for abandoning his children and the nightmares he has caused me. A year of silence is a small price to pay to see him, his gutter woman, and his bastard children brought to their knees. I will be silent till judgment day, if I have to, and then laugh as I watch God pour out his wrath on him and them."

"Who recommended me as an attorney?"

"Your uncle, the Reverend Beecham, told me of you." She replied. "Since meeting him in the cemetery where his wife is buried, we have become letter friends. We pray, share burdens, and discuss Bible topics in our letters. I find him quite interesting and he holds me up in prayer. I do not have an Amish gathering house here to attend. His letters are my church."

"Your friendship with him pleases me, Naomi. My uncle has been seriously lost in his grief. He needs a friend who shares his religious values. The loss of his wife zapped him."

"Your uncle is a wonderful man. He takes me by his letters to exotic lands and tells me of strange peoples I have never heard of. His letters are very exciting. In return, I tell him of my former life as an Amish woman on my farm in Missouri. He wishes to write a book. I am pleased."

"I may want to write one myself when this case is concluded. I haven't had anything this interesting come across my desk in quite some time. I have always wanted to write a novel with me as the main character."

Naomi rose from her seat as did the attorney.

"Goodbye Mr. Maynard."

"I will see you next Monday. Have my receptionist schedule you a time."

Naomi did as she was told and then left the attorney's office to enter a week of silence and waiting.

Standing outside of the Attorney's office invisibly waiting, were Osceola and Frankie Frances. They had been counting cars going by, out of sheer boredom.

"Why did God assign you to this Amish woman and the others we are to accompany after her? A three year old angel could follow this woman around. She is as boring as they come. Other than that itty bitty, imp of a demon last week, there has been no action to protect her from. I was hoping for a little excitement on my first big mission. The only threatening thing I have seen is you yelling at me!" Frankie Frances mouthed as they fell in behind Naomi to follow her as she walked home.

"I am asking myself the same question." Osceola replied biting her lip. She was not happy walking day in and day out behind the white cap who never took a taxi. Her gold stilettos were wearing out and it might be months before she made it to Paris or New York City to purchase new ones. She was going to have it out with the White Suit when she got home. The white cap, in her thinking, was a waste of her time when she could be rescuing dozens of people's souls from floods, volcano eruptions, and storms at sea.

"I could come up with a way to relieve our boredom, if you would not yell at me." Frankie Frances baited her.

"I wouldn't yell at you, if you would learn to zip your lip and practice silence in my presence. I don't like you very much and you don't like me. Talking magnifies our dislike for each other. I am sure that you and I will survive this mission together. However, when it is over, I never want to look at your pimple face or listen to your mouth again. Now, stuff a chocolate bar in your mouth and let me follow Naomi in peace." Osceola stated harshly in her syrupy, sticky, fly killing voice.

"Don't you even want to hear my solution to our boredom problem? Mrs. God would hear me out. You are definitely not much like her. She is nice and bakes me cookies when I am up there walking her dogs. Once she even put some of her denture crème on my nose to keep my glasses from sliding down. Wasn't that nice of her?" Frankie Frances stated pushing her glasses back up her nose and into place.

"Okay . . . okay . . . tell me your idea and then zip your lips. You are giving me a headache with your never ending jaw flapping.

"We need something, a shared unique experience, to make us friendlier toward each other and give us something to giggle and snicker about when we are having our late night talks sitting on the third floor stairs outside of Naomi's apartment, while she sleeps."

"Just get to the point. What do you have in mind?" Osceola asked rolling her eyes.

"What if we take turns taking a night off? Suppose I go one night to a rock concert and the next night you fly up north and spend some stolen moments with your long legged Jack Rabbit man. I am even willing to let you go first." Frankie Frances stated grinning from ear to ear. "If you don't snitch to God, I won't. I cross my heart and hope to die." She stated taking her hand and making a cross in the location of her heart. Behind her back, she had two crossed fingers on her other hand that Osceola did not see.

"Sorry, Frankie Frances, I wouldn't let my own kid go to a rock concert alone at thirteen. Perverts hang out there of all sorts.

"Okay, forget the rock concert. On my night, I will fly to Hershey, Pennsylvania and eat all the chocolate I want and then go to the middle school and throw up in all the girl's toilets. That should be fun. Hershey was my hometown before crossing over."

"Throwing up in the girl's toilets is your idea of a night off?" Osceola asked in disgust.

"Getting even with a boy I once liked who made me cry inferring I had dog-breath is a great night off. That boy is now a school janitor. He can clean up my vomit which will indeed smell like dog breath, if you will let me use your nail file. It has been over thirty years since I crossed over from Hershey. I was in a car wreck. Anyway, that insulting boy is now forty-three and I am not crying." Frankie Frances replied snickering. "Think of your long legged Jack Rabbit and how you could be all wrapped up in his arms and legs and sniffing his after shave . . ."

"We would be in deep . . . for abandoning our post."

"I won't tell God if you don't tell him." Frankie Frances stated all smiles. "Does the idea of being in your long legged Jack Rabbit's arms for one night make you like me any better? We could giggle and snicker about him and my vomit man next week. Don't forget, I am being nice and willing to let you go first."

"You are one devious, little witch of an angel." Osceola replied in her syrupy, sticky, sweet voice. "It is a deal."

CHAPTER FIFTEEN

The Detective's Findings

The following week crept by. Naomi busied herself with her cleaning customers, quilting, baking, and letter writing to keep her-self moving thru it. Even with her efforts to stay busy, a snail could have moved faster than her week of waiting.

Naomi had been extremely afraid all the years since Joel had pushed her down. She had feared that he would return to the farm crazy and kill her with his kicks, not knowing what he was doing. She had not forgotten the dark look in his eyes when he had done so. Now she was in extreme fear because she felt he was not crazy and that his acts had been willful. She feared he would somehow find out where she was before the year was up. She now knew that the darkness in his eyes was his wanting to be free of her. Her children had died because he was not man enough to ask her for a divorce. She had been shunned for the same reason. She had spent five years waiting for him to come home sane for the same reason.

Now, knowing she had discovered his secret, she had a case of jittery nerves. If he had callously pushed her down in a sane moment, not a crazy one, to rid himself of her and her children, he was capable of killing her. She double checked the closet she slept in to make sure her knife was there each night. Also, she put three barrel latches on the inside of her closet door to lock herself in, so she could sleep. She had a year ahead of her and she had to be safe. She had no one to protect her and she had to rely on herself.

Naomi thought of Marcus as she busied herself. She was appalled at herself for her attachment to him. She had to get her emotions under control before facing him again at the market. He was not what he had projected to her he was. He chased married women and his sister and nephew were now her enemies. Satan had tried to trick her and make her fall in love with Marcus. She now knew not to trust anyone, except Jack. Darkness crept upon you in many forms, and she had almost embraced part of it, Marcus.

Turning her back on Marcus was not going to be easy. However, she had to do it. He had lied to her over and over thru the sin of omission. He had never told her he was a professor or that he had a married lady friend named Jenkins. Thru Dan Maynard's words, she had seen him as not having one married friend, but many. He was a sinful, fornicating, adulterous man that put on a good front. He was a good looking Satan and had almost deceived her. She also knew that her friendship with Marcus would end and he would turn on her once her polygamy case hit the news. She had purposely asked Dan Maynard to see that it was widely publicized in the newspaper. She wanted to shame Joel and those involved, as she had been shamed and shunned. An eye for an eye and a tooth for a tooth was God's recompense for evil, and she expected it.

What Naomi had not expected was her jealousy concerning Marcus and his many lady friends. Anger over her racing heart and her naive stupidity gnawed at her. She had let herself believe that a man like him could possibly have feelings for her. Adam Too had been right. She was ugly and, apparently, Marcus had sick reasons for befriending her. She shuddered at the thought that it was possible he just wanted to sleep with her as a married woman; play a game with her. She was thankful she was awakening from her Marcus dream just in time.

Naomi needed a reason to cool her relationship with Marcus and move her booth. Adam Too was probably her best plausible reason for doing so. She would move her table across the aisle at the farmer's market and strike up new friendships. It was time and necessary. Marcus could not be a part of her world now. It was not feasible that he would walk away from his sister, her children, and she didn't want to think about his lady friends. Dan Maynard was right. Blood was thicker than water. She had no intention of walking away from her dead children and let them go un-avenged. He would stand up for his sister and her children.

Naomi thought about her folding table that Marcus carted back and forth for her. She had no way to cart it back and forth. She might have to return to spreading her wares on a table cloth, till she could figure something out. Perhaps the snack shack people would let her slip her table inside their food stand for a couple of weeks. She now had to rethink her way of doing business at the market. Also, Marcus would not now be making her stickers and labels on his computer. Her world was changing. God had helped her to get started in Paducah. She would depend on him to help her do so again without Marcus.

On Saturday, instead of going to the farmer's market, she went shopping for fabric for her new someday quilt. She decided to pretend she was fifteen and not married yet. She would try to remember the innocence and love that was within her at that point and put that into her new someday wedding quilt along with dreams of a special someone coming along who would love her, not abandon her, and not see her as ugly.

Naomi, while shopping for fabric, decided to make a bow tie quilt. English men wore ties and the pattern would be pleasing to a non-Amish man. She was sure she would never return to the Amish community or marry another of its brethren. Her Amish brethren had abandoned and shunned her when she needed them the most. If the Reverend Beecham were younger, she would run a way to Haiti with him and never return. She would visit all the exotic places that her friend had written her about, sleeping each night beneath her new someday quilt. She now had to make herself number one. She knew she was ugly and there was the possibility that no man would ever love her. Adam Too had pointed out that fact to her. His father had also done that by leaving her. Marcus had done so by not making Adam Too apologize to her. Naomi saw herself thru Joel's eyes, an ugly woman not worth keeping. His abandonment of her had stolen her self-worth and years of being a woman and loving someone. She was sure that no holy good man, like the Reverend Beecham, would ever want her. She was a used up, discarded, ugly farm girl.

Monday evening arrived once more and Naomi made her way to her late day attorney's appointment. The receptionist sent her straight on back. She was Mr. Maynard's last appointment for the day.

"Sit down Naomi." Dan Maynard stated pointing to the chair at his desk facing him.

Naomi seated herself and so did he. She watched nervously as he pulled a large brown envelope from his desk drawer and proceeded t o open it and lay its contents face down on his desk.

"I have news, but it is not probably what you were looking for." He stated pausing and tapping his pencil eraser on his desk thinking. "I have a question for you before we start. I feel I have to ask it."

"What is it?" Naomi replied inquiring.

"If I told you that Joel had wandered away from your farm with a mental disease called Schizophrenia and there were no other women in his life; that he just had literally gone off the deep end and was in a state mental hospital in a catatonic state, what would you do?"

"I would go get him and return to the farm with him. Then, I would pray and repent for my dark unwarranted suspicions and take care of him till death took one of us. I married for life and do not believe illness is a reason for divorce. I would forgive him for my children knowing he was truly crazy."

"That is what I thought. You are a good woman, Naomi. I wish your Amish husband had been half the woman you are, but he was not and still is not. He is not Schizophrenia, Naomi. He is far from it and you have a right to a divorce in your God's eyes. Are you ready to look at the contents I have taken from this envelope?"

"Yes, I am ready."

"Just as you suspected, your husband did remarry illegally, but not to Marcus' sister. He married another woman when he wandered away those first two or three times for a day or so from the farm when you were pregnant with Adam. He used a version of his Amish name on the marriage certificate spelling his last name of Toombs backwards. Mrs. Sbmoot has returned to using her maiden name of Cameron, although they are still married. He married her as near as I can tell just weeks after he married you. She refers to him using the nick name of Joey. I am still digging and putting your case together. However, He is definitely married to her and has been so for around eleven years. You were married to him five and then waited five and have been here for over a year."

"He married another woman named Cameron when I was pregnant with Adam?" Naomi asked in shock.

"He married her when you were newly- weds; possibly on one of those three day or so wanderings of his. I haven't worked the exact time line on your case out yet, but he did marry someone else within two or three months of marrying you."

"Why would he return to me and get me pregnant a second time if he had married a second wife?"

"I was shocked at what I found myself. You can thank my secretary for the quick discovery of what your husband has been up to. I didn't even have to pump Jenkins. I gave my secretary all of your information so that she could create a file folder. She recognized your husband's name, although it was spelled in reverse. She read the file as she put it together and recognized your description of him. She attended your husband's wedding to a friend of hers when you were pregnant with Adam."

"Your secretary knows my Joel and his second wife?"

"Joel and his illegal wife lived here in Paducah. The wife still does. They are in the process of divorcing. Are you ready to hear more?"

"Yes, go ahead Mr. Maynard." Naomi stated with all blood draining from her face. She felt sure she knew who the woman named Cameron was, who was getting a divorce from Joel.

"His illegal second wife Karen you know. It is a fluke you living in her apartment house. Anyway, she was happily married and her salesman husband, Joey, was a way on a sales trip supposedly to Chicago. She, looking for something to pass the time, drove down to Nashville to visit a retired teacher friend of hers who had gone into a nursing home. She walked in on her husband and a woman in one of the nursing home's rooms. Her other woman worked there. He played around on Karen just as he did you, only he got a little smarter with his game. Instead of pretending he was crazy with Karen, he passed himself off as a traveling sales man who was only home on weekends. That gave him time to add a third woman on the string. I have a detective working on the case documenting all the details. Are you ready to look at some photos that my secretary provided me with from her personal photo album?"

"Yes. I wish to see." Naomi stated. She burst into tears when he handed her the first one. It was Joel standing by a wedding cake dressed in an English

145

white wedding suit but wearing his Amish beard.

"Is the man in the photo your husband? I want to hear you say it, so we can proceed."

"It is him, Mr. Maynard. It is indeed my husband Joel." She replied taking a tissue he offered her.

Mr. Maynard turned over two more photos. Naomi was shocked looking at a young red headed bride and Joel as the groom kissing her. Naomi looked at a third group photo and recognized a younger version of his secretary dressed as a bride's maid.

"Is that your secretary in the maid of honor dress?"

"Yes, Naomi, it is. Do you recognize anyone else?"

"The skinny, young, red haired bride is my landlord, Karen Cameron." Naomi stated. Karen was heavier now and wore her hair long and in a pony-tail. "I am a blind fool, Mr. Maynard. Her aunt Molly lives possibly three to five miles from my farm, back home. I never suspected, till now, that my and Karen's lives with Joel were running parallel. Joel could have walked away and spent two or three days easily and then walked back in the beginning. Even the city would have only been a four hour walk."

"I was shocked myself, at what I found. You are in a touchy situation, Naomi, and we must keep this case totally on the hush-hush. Your husband and Karen lived in an apartment in that city for the first five years they were married. She was working and putting herself thru the local University. It was easy for him to make his way back to you when he and Karen had spats. The crop money that your husband disappeared with, leaving you with only thirteen or fourteen dollars, was given to Karen for the down payment on the apartment complex here that you live in. It was his way of making up with her. Their last spat in Missouri left them separated for two years."

"My two good years with him were a lie." Naomi stated brushing away a tear.

"He and Karen were split up those two years. She wanted to move here to Paducah after college graduation, and of course he didn't, the reason being that he could not wander back to you when he wanted. So, she told him to take a hike and he returned to you for the two years pretending amnesia. Chances are that he wasn't quite mature yet and willing to give up on the farm, his parents, and his religion which he kept a secret. I imagine one day he decided he wanted her more than you and your Amish world and walked away for good. He wandered back into her life in Paducah trying to impress her with a roll of cash he had on him. They made up and purchased the apartment house. He intentionally took all of your crop money, hurt you, and abandoned your children."

Tears rolled down Naomi's cheeks. What good memories she had were shattered. "Who gave him the male disease he brought home to me, Mr. Maynard? Was Karen a harlot back during the five years?"

"If I were guessing, I would say he brought the disease home to you from someone, other than Karen. He was leaving you in the beginning of your marriage for a day at a time. He was young and experiencing the city. Chances are he slept a few times with what you call harlots. He may have also given the same disease to Karen. Of course, I can't ask her because we are keeping your case hush-hush for now."

"He was not crazy and had no regard for my health."

"He was not interested in you or your marriage, Naomi. Apparently, he wanted a life besides his Amish roots. He embraced that life for a few stolen days, weeks, and then months while he matured. Then one day he made the decision to walk away for good. Are you ready for me to continue?"

"Yes, Mr. Maynard, continue . . ."

"I hired a detective last Monday to start digging. Your husband, Joel, has developed a pattern. You were the first he wandered away from, but there have been several women he has married and abandoned since you. After you was Karen. While in an illegal marriage to her, he entered into more relationships within hours of here. There are a couple of illegal wives in Indiana and Ohio looking for him. More wife leads are popping up. He has stepped up his game and now dumps and abandons them when he gets what he can get from them, or they get suspicious. Karen seems to be the only one he has feelings for. He keeps trying to return to her, each time offering her a roll of cash taken from one of his other victims. You are lucky, Naomi. You are the first and legal wife. The court will award you whatever assets he has. The others are victims of polygamy. '

"I do not know what to say, Mr. Maynard. I waited for five years back in Missouri for him to return thinking he was schizophrenic. I have been here over a year without any word of him."

"Karen, as far as we can tell right now, was wife number two. She gave me Joel's work address in Nashville. My detective was given a tip at a tattoo parlor there taking him to St. Louis. There, he discovered two wives living parallel lives in the same city, who did not know about each other. My private eye has leads on three more women scattered between here and Ohio who may be more polygamy victims. Your husband is getting sloppy and using his real name now with the latest ones. His tattooed body is now making it easy for each victim to identify him just from my detective's oral description. Not many men have nudes tattooed on their bodies. Those, thinking they have found their missing husbands, are falling over backwards giving him information because they all want alimony and child support payments."

"Joel is married to me, Karen, two women in St. Louis, and possibly three more scattered in the north . . . and he has children?"

"Seven possible wives is the current count, Naomi. It is going to take me awhile to accumulate and sort all of the details. Not only is your husband an adulterer, he is a sociopath polygamist."

"You mentioned child support, how many bastard children does he have?"

"This you are not going to want to hear . . ." Dan Maynard stated pausing.

"I want to hear. Go ahead!"

"The current count is seven. All the boys are named Adam or Abraham and the girls are either named Mary or Martha."

"He named my two children Adam and Mary. He tried to replace them."

"Your husband, according to my detective, also has a taste for hookers on the side. Marcus's sister is just one of many prostitutes he frequents. She is probably just sex to him, and him money to her. She is a hooker in Nashville and services hundreds of men. Her son could possibly be your husbands or by hundreds of men she has slept with. The last name of Too is not on Angela's son's birth certificate. Her maiden name is on it, as well as those of her other two children. Your husband has slept with her, but she is probably just paid for sex to him. Anyway, that is the way it looks like now. He is currently living with his two wives in St. Louis."

"So, Marcus's sister and her Adam's mole is just a fluke thing that helped me open my can of worms?"

"Angela probably listened to your Joel speak of your children and his parents when he was visiting her for services. She probably liked the names and just used them. We can have the children DNA tested if you wish. However, she is just a cheap, back alley, twenty dollar tramp in Nashville and not married to your husband. Marcus' sister has nothing materially and will add nothing to our case. She is what she is, a cheap, gutter hooker. The women your husband married, makes up our case.

"I am in total shock, Mr. Maynard. So, you think I should just ignore Angela and Adam Too because Joel really is not a part of their lives, other than he has possibly bought sex from her as has many men?"

"That is my opinion concerning her for now. However, I would cool my friendship with Marcus, Naomi. He is just as bad as she is, just in other ways. A man who chases only married women has a screw loose. Plus, as I have cautioned you, I need you to stay away from all men for the next year."

"You do not have to worry about me, Mr. Maynard. I will do what you tell me. I waited for five years for Joel to return to me and our farm, even though he caused the death of my children. I want you to ask for the clothes on his back and the lint in his belly button. His disrespect of me, as his wife, and his innocent children in the manner he has done so, is unfathomable."

"He had no intention of returning to you, Naomi, when he left the last time. When he left you, taking the crop money, he embraced a new life not giving your or your children's welfare a second thought. A man who loves you, does not take thousands of dollars and give it to another woman leaving you with fourteen dollars and two kids to feed. I am sure he is unaware that your two children are dead and doesn't care. Sociopaths only think of themselves. Karen Cameron is the only wife that he keeps trying to return to. Somewhere inside of his sociopath brain, he may actually have some feelings for her. However, right now he seems to be content wandering back and forth between the two wives in St. Louis."

"Does Marcus' sister know about his many wives?"

"Marcus' sister sells her body to men for money. She services all sorts of men. She is a cheap twenty dollar whore and he probably returns to her when he is short of funds. However, according to my detective, she hasn't seen him for months and may never again. He has some wealthier wives on the hook and may be moving up to higher paid call girls."

"Karen Cameron and I have befriended each other. Did she know about me when she married Joel?"

"My secretary says Karen was aware that her Joe had been married before back in Missouri. He was still wearing his Amish dress and beard when he met her. He told her that he was freshly divorced and had just left his Quaker roots in Ohio moving to Missouri and intended to become a salesman and live as the English did. He lied to her and she fell for it. He never mentioned you or your Amish settlement."

"What must I now do about Karen? I live beneath her roof and pay her rent."

"For the next year, you are to continue living in your apartment and act like nothing is wrong. I will tell you when they are going to surprise and serve Joel with his divorce papers in St. Louis. He will immediately call Karen wanting his half of the apartment complex and promise her anything to get it before he tries to disappear. I will let you know when to walk away from the apartment. Be prepared to walk away quickly, carrying what is important to you. Act normal for now, till I get your case together and an arrest warrant is served on your husband for polygamy. We will make a case and charge him with the murder of your daughter later. For now, we just want him in jail, till our case goes to court. We want him to go on as normal in St. Louis till we are ready. We don't want him running. Don't rock your boat, Naomi. Remember your dead children and do exactly as I say. You must remain silent and act normal for a year, till I tie up all the loose ends of your case and we go to court."

"How about your secretary, will she warn Karen?"

"Karen was her friend years ago. However, my secretary Edna is a straight-laced Bible thumping Baptist. Joel hit on her and tried to sleep with her behind Karen's back. She refused him and Joel broke up her and Karen's friendship by telling Karen it was Edna hitting and flirting with him. Edna is like you; she has morals and lives by them. She is on God's side, which is your side. Karen dumped her and their friendship years ago."

"It is hard for me to face that my Joel is a womanizer."

"Not a womanizer, Naomi. He is a woman user. There is a difference. Joel does not love the women or the children he has by them. He is a user, a man who plays games with women."

"How many other children do you really think he has, besides mine?" She couldn't help but asking.

"The current count is possibly nine children scattered between the different wives. If we count Adam Too the count would be ten. However, we want to stick to the ones born to the women he married."

"We had a big farm back in Missouri and I thought our life was good. His parents lived next to us and doted on him and our son Adam. What was missing that he would turn to darkness like this?"

"My secretary knows your husband better than anyone we know, right now. I am not approaching Karen about this. She is to be kept in the dark, the same as the other wives till court. Edna says your husband had a passion for art. My detective tells me that Joel now works in St. Louis as a tattoo artist and on the side paints canvases with nudes on them that he sells to bars, etc. His physical body now has multiple nude women tattooed on it. Once he crossed the line, and started tattooing his body with naked women, he probably knew he could no longer return to you. His nude body paintings would not be acceptable in your Amish world."

"Graven images are not allowed in the Amish community. His mother once told me she switched him when he was little for drawing horses on the inside of her outhouse walls. His father once caught him drawing birds in the loft of his family's barn and also disciplined him for it. His father burned his drawings in front of him before paddling his backside. It is appalling to me that he would abandon me and our two children for graven images. I, personally, would not have cared if he painted in the attic of our home. I lean a little toward being modern Amish. It hurts me that he hid his love of art from me. I quilt and that is art!"

"There may still be some of his early paintings stored in the basement of the apartment house where you live. My secretary says he used to paint down there before Karen threw him out."

"I will secretly look when I get a chance." Naomi replied.

"Edna, my secretary, has been with me for twelve or so years. She is an art lover and does volunteer work in her spare time at the Art Museum and is a volunteer member of their board of directors. Joel towards the end of his marriage to Karen, wanted Edna's connections. He tried to seduce Edna. In his thinking, Edna was the connection he needed to get his canvases shown in the museums modern art gallery. Edna told him to take a hike, she also tried to tell Karen about his attempt to seduce her. Karen was blindly in love with him and dumped Edna as a friend believing your Joel's lies about Edna trying to seduce him. He uses women to get what he wants and he doesn't care who gets in his way or who he hurts."

"What a blind cow I have been. He was creating a new life for himself in his wanderings from the farm, knowing he planned to abandon me eventually. He had no feelings for me or my children."

"He doesn't care about the other women's children either. In his sick little world of deceit, the only two people he loves are himself and Karen for some reason."

"I have never met Marcus' sister. What is she like?"

"She is a street hooker with an out of control, weight problem. She probably weighs three hundred pounds. I will ask the detective to photograph her, so you will know what she looks like, should she show up here for any reason. Don't approach her if she does. She is a criminal and has a long record of hooking, assaults, petty theft, and the destruction of other people's property, if she is crossed. She is the woman that Karen walked in on with her husband in the nursing home in Nashville. I am surprised the windows in Karen's apartment house have survived. Breaking car and house windows seems to be a thing with her. Just be careful and if you see a very large woman with a buzz cut between now and the time I get you a photo, turn and walk the other way. She is a very low class, gutter rat of a woman who wouldn't think twice about robbing you just because she wanted your white cap to use to blow her nose on."

"So you think Adam Too is just a fluke, a bastard child with no known father and Angela gave him Joel's name just because she liked it?"

"He could be Joel's or the offspring of a hundred others she might have slept with the week she conceived. It is a crap shoot."

"Why would my Joel leave Karen who is respectable to live with a gutter rat, harlot woman?"

"He did not leave Karen. She threw him out after catching him with Marcus' sister in Nashville. I am guessing Joe was suddenly without money and conned the hooker into letting him stay with her till he found two higher class women to con in St. Louis. His well with Karen dried up. Angela is probably just a fly speck on the wall paper of his world."

"I would like to say that I am sad for Karen and the others. However, I am not. Karen and the harlot used money I sweated for working the farm fields. I worked in the fields pregnant with both Adam and Mary. They have not had a daughter lying in their arms in seizures, dying. They have not buried two children in one week with no money to buy them a proper headstone. They have not been shunned by their friends or communities."

"There is no need to feel sorry for anyone, Naomi. The prostitute has no morals and Karen Cameron is a professional who should have know better than to marry a man she didn't know. She should have had Joel, whom she calls Joey, checked out. You were an orphan when you married Joel and had no one to look out for your best interests. You are lucky that you are not dead at his hands. You were simply a way for him to get out from under the thumb of his parents. Someone probably told him about Amnesia and he hatched a plan of acting crazy to get to wander away to the city and do what he wanted. As he matured in his twenties, he just made the decision to never return to you and moved on to others who could get him where he wanted to go, which was far away from you and your Amish world."

"I was almost sixteen and he was seventeen when we married. I lost Mary when I was twenty. He abandoned us for good when he was twenty-two and I was twenty. Now it is six going on seven years later. I have wasted the best years of my life on him. I am now, almost twenty-seven."

"Don't look at it like wasting the best years of your life, Naomi. Look at it like the best years of your life are just now beginning. Go home. Keep our secrets for a year. Live your new life well and forget Joel till I call you on the phone or send you word telling you to leave Karen's apartments that we are going to court. If I were you, I would start a journal and start writing about the hell you have been thru. Your story is big enough to be published in book form. You write it and I will attempt to help you get it published when this is all over."

"Thank you, Mr. Maynard. I wish to put my nightmare behind me, not be known for it. It saddens me that Karen will hate me afterward. I honestly did not know her Joey and my Joel were the same man. Marcus has been my friend also. Blood is thicker than water as you say. I am sure that after Joel is arrested he will see me as a deceitful, vengeful woman who has used him for information and attacked his family."

"When the dust settles, Naomi, the friends who stand at your side, are truly your friends. Whoever fails to stand by you, are not who you want in your future new life. I and Edna will be standing next to you when all Hell breaks loose. Whoever else stands with you, are your friends."

"Thank you, Mr. Maynard. I will indeed make note of those standing with me on my husband's judgment day."

Frankie Frances sat invisibly in the vacant office chair next to Naomi. Osceola had not returned from her overnight trip up north to pop in on her long legged Jack Rabbit man. Frankie Frances was all smiles thinking how devious and smart she had been. Getting rid of Osceola had been easy. Now was her big chance to prove herself as an angel and what she was capable of. She had been guarding Naomi alone for two days now. This was her chance. Her one itsy, bitsy, mistake was that she had forgot that Osceola had melted and discarded her nail file sword. She should have asked Osceola to borrow hers while she was away. She hadn't thought about that. However, it didn't matter. Naomi was boring and nothing serious ever happened to her. She could get by without a sword.

Frankie Frances felt a little remorse for tricking Osceola, but not much; maybe Naomi's thimble full. She had tried being nice to Osceola. Osceola wasn't open to niceness. Playing into Osceola's weakness for her Jack Rabbit man, had worked. She had gotten rid of the syrupy, sticky voiced woman who stood in her way of success. She was really pleased with herself and just knew that Osceola had to be rotting upstairs in God's jail cells waiting for an audience to explain herself. She had personally called God's Military police angels and told them that Osceola was away without leave, had abandoned her mission, and was headed for the long legged Jack Rabbit's place. It might take her years to make it back to Earth. By that time, she would have proven herself, guarding the settlement of Amish women, with Naomi being the first who needed her services.

Frankie Frances listened very carefully to every word that Naomi's lawyer said. She was going to perform her angel duty to perfection and not let anything slip by her. This was her big chance to become a guardian angel which allowed you to travel all over Earth experiencing different cultures and shopping. She loved shopping. Her closet back in Heaven was full of school uniforms and dog walking clothes. She was ready for designer clothes and stilettos, just like Osceola. What she hated was walking stinky mutts who did their business anywhere they pleased leaving it for her to clean up with a pooper scooper. She was not a pooper scooper angel. She was a fly me around the world girl and let me take my breaks in the world's malls. This was her chance to make her dream come true. She was going on fourteen and in her thinking old enough to be a full-fledged guardian. Watching the white cap in a gray dress was a piece of cake and she was on her way up the job ladder.

Meanwhile, up In God's Eternal Garden, Osceola Black Lightning stood waiting for her dreaded audience with God or the White Suit as she called him. She had been tricked into leaving her post by a thirteen year old imp of an angel, she called Frankie Frances. She was seething mad. God's military police had caught up with her just as she was about to knock on her long legged Jack Rabbit's door. She was so close to being in his arms that she could feel them when a huge, yellow skinned angel, dressed in camouflage, grabbed her and whisked her off to Heaven after relieving her of her nail file. She hadn't even got a chance to look at her Jack Rabbit's white skin and baby blue eyes. If she ever got a hold of Frankie Frances, she would give her a case of boils and pimples that she would never get cleared up. Leaning on a flowering Magnolia, she waited.

"Well, well . . . if it isn't my favorite death angel. What are you doing here? Did my dog walker get to you and make you flee your post with your tail between your legs, like the dogs she walks?"

"Me . . . flee my post? You have got to be kidding. That imp, you sent me for an assistant, tricked me. She gave me the night off to go see my friend the Jack Rabbit and then called your military police telling them I had abandoned my post. You just wait till I get my hands on her. She is going to pay, White Suit. She is going to pay!"

"Better your problem than mine. You asked for her and she is a no return."

"You are not mad at me for taking a night off? There was an angel there to take my place and guard the white cap." Osceola asked letting her southern voice drip with syrup and sugar.

"Well, it is like this. Before sending her to you, she took a pooper scooper to Mrs. God's tulip bulbs thinking they were poop left by the hounds. Mrs. God was not a happy camper when she had to dig thru a black bag of two week old Hound crap to retrieve them. The day before that, she tied all the dogs to the Eastern Gate while she took a break and went for ice cream. We had a back up of fifty thousand souls who couldn't get in to Heaven due to the hounds of Heaven barking, snarling, and nipping at any one stepping one foot up to the gate. I had to send half of those souls back down just to get the mess at the gate straightened out. Can you imagine what stories they are going to tell about their experience of walking up to Heaven's Gate?"

"She backed up soul traffic that bad . . .?" Osceola asked sympathizing with God by making her voice drip with honey.

"I'm not thru. Last week she lost her glasses and thought a group of demons, waiting at the judgment seat to be sent to the lake of fire, were dogs. She leashed them and walked them right out of the judgment hall to the edge of Heaven and let them fall off a cloud and back down to Earth. I have a military unit out now, trying to recapture them."

"I think I might have run into one of those wimpy little demons last Saturday. He was hiding out in the farmer's market in Paducah. He was a mean little rascal who was traveling in a little boy's body. A skunk came wandering thru the market. I got distracted and the little imp got away from me. I will try to recapture him for you next Saturday." Osceola replied trying to butter the White Suit up.

"The military police will recapture them. What I want you to concentrate on is those Amish women and keeping Frankie Frances out of my hair. You are the only angel I have that is sassy enough to deal with her. I have to forgive you because I don't want her back." He stated and then went to laughing. "You do know she is down there guarding Naomi without a sword?"

"Oops, . . . I forgot about taking hers from her. Am I in trouble for that?" Osceola asked in her syrupy, sticky, southern slow voice.

"Not as long as you return to your post and keep that dog walking disaster out of my Heaven and my Garden. I don't want her back up here till she is at least forty. She drives everybody up here crazy." He said handing her nail file sword back to her.

"She got to you too, White Suit, didn't she?" Osceola asked suddenly all smiles. "What did she do?"

"I have forgiven her and her sins against me. They are in my sea of forgetfulness. Now, get back down there to your Amish Post and take care of that Frankie Frances, companion gift I sent you. You asked for her."

"You are not a very nice man, White Suit. I asked you to send me a companion or an assistant because I was lonely. I didn't ask for a pain in the butt." Osceola retorted in a mad, syrupy, sticky, fly swatting voice moment.

"Okay, so I fudged a little when I answered your request. Could you just keep her out of my hair till I solve my angel shortage? I do not have time to deal with her and her antics right now." God replied with a smirk on his face."Plus, I am afraid to let her shine my shoes."

Osceola went to laughing. "Better your shoes than mine!"

"Get out of here!" God retorted.

CHAPTER SIXTEEN

The First Day of Forever

After her appointment with her attorney, Naomi returned home to her apartment and locked herself into her closet to think. She felt like she was in a numb haze. She lay down on her pallet in the dark and tried to make sense of everything Dan Maynard had told her. Joel had never loved her or considered their marriage to be sacred and forever. In the dark, she cried, prayed, and in a state of exhaustion fell asleep.

After avoiding the farmer's market for two Saturdays, Naomi felt she had her emotions and feelings for Marcus under control. So, she packed her rolling tote and headed for the farmer's market. On the way, she rehearsed any answers she might need to give, as to why she had not been there. Nearing the market, Marcus did not run to meet her. Entering the market, she saw that he was busy conversing with a blond headed woman who had claimed her booth spot in her absence next to him. That she had not expected.

As she neared her spot, she saw that a tall lanky blonde in jeans and a ball cap had a display of cactus plants set up on her folding table.

Shortly before Naomi's arrival, Marcus had set up his milk crates and Naomi's card table in hopes she would show up. As he was finishing, Professor Jenkins got out of a cab with a cardboard container of small pots of cactus. She walked immediately over to the spot next to Marcus and set her cactus down.

"What are you doing here?" He demanded in a surprised voice. He knew that Naomi could be there any moment and he did not want the two of them to meet.

"Just pretend I am selling cactus for the morning. Something fishy is going on and I need to talk to you. I will catch a cab back home afterward."

"I don't understand. What do you need to talk to me about? We haven't been seeing each other for months." He quickly replied wanting to get rid of her. He did not want Naomi to know about his past.

"A man showed up out at my house late last evening asking me questions about your sister, very personal questions. How he knew you and I had a thing going, I don't know. Are you and your sister in some sort of trouble?"

"You know me better than that, Jenkins. I want a respectable life. That is the whole focus of my being here, escaping from my religious nut mother and my whore of a sister."

"Well then, your sister has pulled something pretty serious or they wouldn't be tracking down your ex lady friends and pumping them for information. The man said he was a detective and he wanted to know if I knew who the father was of your sister's children. Maybe they are from social services and they are going to finally step in and take the kids for good."

"Thanks for telling me Jenkins. I guess I had better think about putting up some bunk beds and a crib at my place. Maybe she has broken her latest probation?"

"I don't know why they are interested in me. I am not happy about being dragged into whatever is going on. Charlie doesn't know anything about you or your sister. I was just lucky he ran last night to gas up his car and pick us up some dinner. I insisted that the detective drive down to the river to talk. I met him down there. He had the gall to ask me if I had ever been out with your sister's tattoo man. I was furious."

"I am sorry, Jenkins. I don't know what is going on, but I will find out and put a stop to it. Did the detective give you a card or a number?"

Jenkins reached into her jeans pocket and pulled out a business card and handed it to him. He was shocked when he looked at it.

"You know the detective and so do I. That is why I am warning you. Your vendor booth friend, Jack, has apparently been here in the market for reasons other than selling produce. Why is he watching me and you?"

"Your husband, Jenkins . . . It has to be your husband. He has probably hired Jack to follow you. He is probably trying to build a divorce case. Jack knows about you and me. I thought we were friends until now."

"That S.O.B., he left on purpose last night so the detective could shake me down."

"Your husband is probably trying to link you to my sister's filth to make you look bad. I am really sorry." Marcus quickly stated and slipped Jack's detective agency card in his back jeans pocket. "You had better get out of here, before he thinks you and I are on again."

"Take these cactus and just pitch them in a trash can when I am gone. I will stay for a couple hours pretending to sell them, so I have a legitimate excuse for being here."

"All right . . . You ignore me and I will ignore you. I promise you I will straighten out whatever the problem is." Marcus stated and then stepped over into the area of his gourd booth and stayed there.

Arriving in front of her old vendor booth spot, Naomi was instantly angry. She bit her lip trying to control her unexpected feelings. It had not taken Marcus long to replace her. A blonde in a ball cap now occupied her booth space and her card table. Although seething, she smiled and said good morning to the blonde and then to Marcus and claimed one of two vacant spots across from them. At least she was able to relocate her vendor booth without having to explain her choice to him for doing so. That was a blessing she told herself.

Marcus was instantly across the center aisle taking her rolling tote from her and helping her sit down a tote bag of bread she was carrying.

"I didn't think you were coming back! I am sorry, I loaned her your table. I will make you a display out of my milk crates with a board stretched across." He quickly stated knowing from the look on Naomi's face he was in the dog house.

"There will be no need. I will spread my checked table cloth on the ground.

Your lady friend must pay me two dollars an hour for the use of my table. I am a business woman. Eight hours will be sixteen dollars."

"Naomi . . . Don't embarrass the hell out of me or make a scene right now. I have got problems and don't refer to her as my lady friend." He said pulling out his billfold. "I will pay her table rent. She only plans to stay for a couple of hours."

"Put your billfold away, Marcus. You loaned something that was not yours to loan. Either you tell her, or I will walk across the aisle and claim my table. Your money is not acceptable. The table is mine and the terms of renting it is mine, also." Naomi replied not smiling.

Naomi was fuming on the inside that Marcus had replaced her so easily. Her husband Joel had also replaced her easily. In the moment she made up her mind to never let another man walk on her. Marcus' loaning of her table, without her permission, in her mind was walking on her. Marcus just like Joel had taken what was hers and given it to another. That was not happening. She could not reclaim the crop money that was taken from her that she had labored in the fields for, but she could reclaim her table that she had sold bread to pay for.

"Please Naomi, don't embarrass me. She doesn't know about our . . . our friendship. I will pay you double the eight hours."

"On my first day at the market here, I displayed my items on the ground. I gather you feel she is above me, an ugly, plain, farm girl and deserving of my table. I paid you for the table. Now she must pay me or give it to me."

"You are trying to embarrass me because of Adam, aren't you? The woman with the cactus is my friend."

"I thought I was." Naomi replied.

"You are more than a friend." He half whispered. "Now, please back off. Jack is watching."

"You have in two weeks easily replaced me and have the gall to give my table to another. I am not trying to embarrass you. I am just standing up for myself. You did not stand up for me when your Adam was disrespecting me with his mouth. You made no effort to have him say he was sorry to me. I no

161

longer need you to stand up for me and what is mine. The table is mine and I will stand up for myself."

"You are the most exasperating woman that I have ever met, next to my Victorian mother. I will not tell her." He stated stomping off across the aisle to his booth, thinking she wouldn't do anything.

Naomi knew that he thought she wouldn't have the nerve to do anything about the table just as she had done nothing about Adam bad mouthing her. He thought he had just won their war of words. She knew that if she didn't stand up for herself and claim her table, it would be like letting Joel push her in the floor again. Only this time, it would be Marcus pushing her and her table was her baby. Breathing deep, the Amish did not believe in confrontation, she stepped across the center aisle walkway and faced the bleached blonde wearing a ball cap. She ignored Marcus whose mouth dropped open.

"I am sorry, but Marcus has misinformed you. The table you have your display on is mine and I wish to use it myself today. Please remove your items from it."

"Naomi . . . !" Marcus shouted coming to the blonde woman's aid. "I loaned it to her. I didn't think you would be here. Be a good sport about this!"

"I will be a good sport. No man walks on me. Buy your lady friend here her own table. This one is mine."

"Who is this bitch, Marcus?" The blonde in the ball cap asked. "Are you going to let her stand there and call me your lady friend knowing what we do?

Naomi looked Marcus in the eye to see what his reaction was.

"It will be okay. Naomi is a vendor and she is mad at me over some words my nephew said to her a couple of weeks ago. I will take care of the problem." He replied to the blonde and turned to Naomi once more. "Back off Naomi, you are making a fool out of yourself." He stated reaching for her arm to pull her away from Jenkins and her table of cactus."

"You will take your hand off of me, Marcus. You do not have the right to touch me in any shape or form. If you don't, I will press charges in court for you assaulting me. In the Amish faith no man can touch me except my husband. Your hand on my arm in my world; is assault." She stated standing

162

her ground and staring him down. He let go of her arm.

"Back off Naomi!" He growled once more.

"Back off?" Naomi retorted in an angry voice upset that he would dare stand against her. "You want me to back off and let your lady friend have my table?"

"Yes, back off! Be an adult about this."

"I am an adult woman who is tired of being walked on and disrespected by men like you and your nephew. You back off, Marcus!"

"Naomi, please . . ." Marcus stated seeing the fire in her eyes.

"I am a non-violent woman no more. Take your lady friend and her wares and shove them up where the sun doesn't shine. A new English friend of mine has taught me that phrase. I believe it is appropriate for your world." She stated. Then reaching quickly, she grabbed the edge of her table and flipped it before he could stop her. The blonde's box of cactus flew everywhere.

Immediately, the irate blonde in the ball cap reached out and slapped Naomi.

"Oh God . . . you didn't!" Marcus stated grabbing the blonde's arm as Naomi stumbled backwards.

"Cat Fight . . . !" one of the male vendors yelled.

Everyone, not having customers, came running to find Marcus standing between two women who were intent on getting at each other. Marcus gave Naomi a slight push into the arms of another male vendor telling him to hold her for a moment. He then quickly took Jenkins in his arms and escorted her to the back of his booth and then helped her into the passenger side of his jeep. Naomi grabbed her card table and carried it across the center of the market quickly and sat it up in her new spot and spread her red checked table cloth on it. Marcus' vendor friend, Jack, who was a detective during the week, immediately started moving his display across the aisle of the market and sat up his display next to Naomi. He was also Naomi's friend.

"You just might need me today, Naomi. If it is okay with you, I will eat

Marcus' apple fritter."

"Thank you, Jack. I appreciate your standing with me. I now know that you are truly my friend. You do realize Marcus is going to be teed off at you for doing so." Naomi replied starting to help him set up his display which he seemed really pleased about.

Marcus left with Jenkins in his jeep and returned about an hour later to find that he not only had lost Naomi as a booth neighbor, but also Jack his fellow neighbor vendor on the other side of him. He looked across the center aisle and saw Jack and Naomi having morning coffee and his friend was eating his fritter. He was pissed. Between Adam and Jenkins, he had alienated the woman he was in love with. She was now across the aisle and had replaced him with his best vendor friend.

Naomi ignored Marcus and did not look his way. She concentrated on selling her goods and chatting with Jack when the customers slowed.

When Marcus was busy with his gourd seeds, Naomi whispered to Jack. "I appreciate your support. My friendship with Marcus is over. Do you intend to reclaim your old spot next Saturday next to Marcus?"

"Why would I do that, when I can sit up over here next to the prettiest woman in this place? I think I will just stay over here with you and watch old Marcus fume about the one that got away before he ever caught her." He whispered back snorting. "You bring me a fritter next week, just to piss him off."

"I will indeed! I stand by friends who stand by me. You bring the coffee."

"You have got it, pretty lady. That blonde bimbo, Jenkins, he brought to the market is a dog next to you."

"She is his lady friend, the married one?"

"Yes, Sweet Thing. She is the one. They must be rolling in the hay again, otherwise she wouldn't be here."

"What am I going to do about my table, Jack? I cannot tote it back and forth."

"I will ask the snack shack vendor to let you put in inside their lockup shack for this week. Next week, I will bring you a short heavy chain and a padlock. You can chain and lock it to the pole. I would take it home with me, but I am on a big case right now and there may be some Saturdays, I might not be here."

"That will work. Thank you! I am most thankful you have stood by me. I was wrong, you know. I should have been nice about the table. My nerves were already on edge when I arrived here this morning. You know why."

"Yes, I know why." He replied reaching down and squeezing her hand. "Personally, I think you could have taken the blonde bimbo if Marcus hadn't stepped between the two of you. I would definitely have bet my money on you." He stated grinning and pouring her some coffee from his thermos.

"You would have lost your money. She was two heads taller than me and got in the first slap. I was at a disadvantage."

Jack laughed. "You may have lost, but you had the guts to pick the fight."

Naomi laughed.

"Thank you again for standing beside me, Jack. I will not forget. How are you and Karen. I have been so wrapped up in myself and my problems, I have failed to ask. I am sorry."

"We have been to the movies two or three times. I was up front with her about my surgery and she is fine with my being incapacitated as a man for awhile."

"I must scold you. Being a man is not about using what has been given you physically. Being a man is being there for a woman when she needs you. You were a man when you stood up for me today. It is how you treat a woman that makes her really love you. A roll in the English hay is just a roll in the hay. Hearts filled with respect and admiration for each other last forever."

"Sweet Thing, you know how to bring the best out of me. I love you for it." He stated reaching down once more and squeezing her hand. "I will pass on to Karen what you said." He knew that as long as he included Karen and she thought that he was taken, she would continue to let him in her world and let him squeeze her hand, which was a stretch for her.

"I am sure Karen will have plenty of advice of her own to pass on to you."

"I love that red head to pieces, but sometimes I think I am going to have to wear ear muffs. She sure loves to run at the mouth."

"She is a talker." Naomi snickered.

"Naomi, I want to thank you once more for helping me last winter in my time of need. When the chips were down and I had no family to turn to, you were there for me. You are guaranteed I will be there for you when you need me, no questions asked."

"Thank you, Jack. We are both alone in this world without family."

"No, Naomi. We are a family of two who have found our way home to Sunday Dinner with each other."

"How are you feeling now?" She asked.

"I am back to work, although I am missing your coffee and cinnamon rolls in the morning."

"Say that quietly!" She stated putting her finger to her lips. "I do not wish anyone to know that I had a man in my apartment for awhile. I am Amish and that is forbidden."

"You kicked me out as soon as I was well! I think your honor is in-tact." He laughed.

"Jack, are you really in love with Karen?"

"Not as much as I am with you. Why, Sweet Thing?" He asked.

"You may tell me no and I will understand. I have the nervous jitters and I am frightened to sleep in my apartment now that I know Joel owns half of the building. Would you let me secretly sleep at your apartment on your couch? I put three dead bolts on my closet door last night and still I could not sleep. I promise to not look out of any of your windows or bring shame to you by letting your neighbors know you have a woman in your place. I need you, Jack. I am scared."

"Well, Sweet Thing, whatever I have is yours, no questions asked. I will sleep on the couch, you get the bed. I can't have my best girl not getting a good night's sleep."

"Your bed is a very big one. Suppose we put pillows down the center between us. I will sleep on one side and you the other." She replied. "I can't have my best fellow not getting a good night's sleep. He is just getting over surgery."

"If I get afraid in the night, will you hold my hand?" He asked and then quickly added. "I was afraid the night I went to surgery, and you held my hand."

"If I am afraid in the night, will you hold me and not my hand?" She asked.

"Are you asking what I think you are asking?" He inquired taking his hand and turning her face up to him.

"I don't want to be alone anymore, Jack. I want arms to hold me. I trust you."

"Sweet Thing, I knew you trusted me when you let me use your tooth brush. I have just been waiting for you to figure out that you want to be in my arms, not Marcus'." He stated.

She smiled at him and squeezed his hand and everything seemed to suddenly be right in her world.

He then leaned down and whispered in her ear. "I want to kiss you, Sweet Thing, but we are in the middle of the farmer's market and you have a divorce case pending. I will always do what is best for you; that includes not kissing you."

She whispered back. "I have not been with a man for six or seven years. You will not be disappointed in me, will you? I am not sure I know how to please an Englishman."

"Sweet Thing, it is me that fears I will not please you." He stated in a whisper and then returned to his vendor booth all smiles. She had discovered that it was him that loved her.

Naomi smiled as she returned to her own booth display. She was happy about the decision she had made. Jack had never failed to be there for her and that was love. When Marcus pushed her into the arms of one of the male vendors and escorted Jenkins out in his arms, her feelings for him died. He had pushed her, just like Joel had pushed her. She would hold close and love the man who always stood beside her. She was ready to love again and have arms hold her. It would just have to be a secret love for the next year.

All had calmed down in the market and the cat fight was history. Jack and Naomi exchanged occasional smiling glances knowing that their first night together later, would be the first of their forever.

For some strange reason, Naomi felt really sleepy for the rest of the day and yawned repeatedly.

So where was Naomi's invisible guardian, Frankie Frances when the cat fight was on?

Peeping out from under Naomi's card table with the check table cloth hanging down part way, a teary eyed frightened Frankie Frances bit her lip and tried to not be noticed. When her white cap got in a cat fight, she had been too afraid to help her, and she didn't have her sword to send the blonde cactus woman flying backwards. Tears rolled down her face. What was she going to do now? She was a failure as a guardian angel. She couldn't just fly back to Heaven abandoning the white cap. Maybe God would understand. Walking dogs wasn't so bad. Maybe God would take her back and let her resume her old position. It was worth a try. Dog fights she could handle, but cat fights were a whole different category. Cats were clawing, vicious, little animals.

"Frankie Frances." A familiar sticky, syrupy voice yelled loudly. Osceola Black Lightning was walking down the center aisle of the farmer's market looking for her.

Frankie stuck her head out from under the card table and forced herself to smile with all her teeth showing from ear to ear. She then pushed her glasses back up on her nose where they belonged and greeted her death angel friend.

"Are you looking for me? I was just under here dozing for a few moments. I broke up a wild, cat fight earlier between your white cap cat and a blond tailed dog. You should have seen how that blonde tailed dog stood on her hind feet and growled like a demon. Anyway, afterward I was drained from the physical altercation and felt I needed a little nap." (When Frankie Frances did not have her glasses pushed up where she could see out of them, humans looked like dogs.)

Osceola reached down with one black arm and snatched Frankie Frances from beneath the card table and stood her up on her feet roughly. She then pointed and swished her long metal nail file at the Cheshire cat, fake grinning girl and gave her one of the biggest pimples a thirteen year old ever had. Osceola was not happy with the White Suit for sending her back to the white caps and for sticking her once more with her teen angel nightmare. She was even angrier about Frankie Frances' tricking her and then her being so close, but not getting to see her long legged Jack Rabbit.

"What did you do that for?" Frankie Frances asked feeling a sore spot form on her face. Then she began to cry. "I will never catch a boy friend with pimples. Couldn't you have made me stand in a corner or given me something less vile?"

"No Jack Rabbit for me, no boyfriend for you." Osceola retorted in her syrupy, sticky, fly swatting voice.

~　　~　　~

Does Naomi get justice for her two dead children? Is Joel arrested for polygamy? What happens to Frankie Frances and her dreams of being a guardian angel? Does Marcus' love for Naomi die? To find out what happens next, read book two of the BLACK LIGHTNING Series.

Also by Jo Hammers

Black Lightning Series, Book 2, Naomi's Dream

Black Lightning Series, Book 3, The Caged Wife

Black Lightning Series, Book 4, The Amish Witch's Quilt

Black Lightning Series, Book 5, The Night Traveler

Black Lightning Series, Book 6, Coffins and Cadavers

Black Lightning Series, Book 7, Ribbons of Darkness

Black Lightning Series, Book 8, Zook's Place

ORDER THIS SERIES FROM

www.paranormalcrossroads.com

www.ingramcontent.com/pod-product-compliance
Lightning Source LLC
Chambersburg PA
CBHW060821120626
46557CB00001B/318